Happy Birth day

Best Wishes,

Gloria Pitchell

2015

THE DARK AND THE LIGHT SIDE OF THE MOON

GLORIA AVAK PITCHELL

ISBN-10: 1502724294
ISBN-13: 978-1502724298

In Memory Of My Parents

Virginia (Mollis) Avak

&

George Avak Achjian

DEDICATED TO:

My husband, Jim

Our children, Jay and Maria

Jeff and Betsy

Our grandchildren,

James

Skyler

Taylor

Sofia

Julia

Jilian

PROLOGUE

Turkey 1911

Near midnight between sleep and consciousness, Avak heard horses' hooves galloping ferociously to the rhythm of Turkish 'dumb a' drums. He was confused; were the soldiers coming upon him or was he dreaming?

He sat up in bed just as his mother burst into his room. In a wild panic she grabbed him by the hand and dragged him to a hidden spot under the wooden porch.

"Stay here, don't move, and don't make a sound," she whispered franticly.

"No," Avak cried, "Stay here with me. The terrified look on her face frightened him. "Why are you leaving me here by myself?" he begged, digging his fingers into her arm.

Agavni pried herself from her son. She cupped his face in her trembling hands and looked into his eyes with a mother's desperate love. She kissed him gently and fiercely at the same time, whispering, "I will always love you. My heart is within your heart, forever." She kissed him gently as her tears covered his cheeks, she pressing one hand on his heart and the other on hers. Then she disappeared.

He shivered and squatted down deeper into the bare ground. He could smell the acrid earth beneath him. The hoof beats were so explosive now he bent down deeper against the soil and covered his ears.

The horses' thunder stopped. Then he felt the vibrations of heavy footsteps on the porch above him. Trembling, Avak lifted his chin, peering upwards through the slats above his head. There were four Turkish soldiers, about the same ages as his brothers, on his porch. He could see them clearly as the moon was bright. They were disheveled and grubby. Only one was wearing high boots, the others, high socks. They wore fezzes made of khaki matching their uniforms. The one with the high boots had a red collar. Avak thought he must be the captain. They pounded down the door and stomped into the house.

In a matter of minutes the four savages dragged his mother, father and two older brothers to the yard away from the house, holding the men at bay with their glistening, menacing sabers. He swallowed hard, folding his hands to his forehead, not wanting to, but compelled to watch. "Oh God, oh God, no, no." he prayed.

His father cried out, "What do you want? Don't touch her. Stop, stop!" as the captain dragged and pushed his mother from the house until she fell to the ground. He pleaded and begged, "I beg of you, please leave her alone. Please don't bring harm to her." His father was held back by two soldiers with sabers at his neck.

The captain dragged her by the hair and ripped off her night gown, got on top of her and proceeded to attack her.

Pitifully trying to fight them off, blood gushing from her mouth, she screamed, "Nazor, help me!" The filthy hand of the captain covered her mouth as he continued. Nazor and his sons watched while screaming. "God help us! Someone help us!"

When the captain was finished, with a contorted smirk, he turned to the other soldiers for each to have his turn. "Hey you Armenians, watch what we do to your woman, just watch!" Agavni's family watched this torturous attack in unadulterated shame. They had to try to do something.

In a futile attempt they lunged at the Turks. One soldier with violent eyes came from behind and drove a sword through their father's hand. He fell to the ground, grimacing with pain; rolling over in dire anguish holding his wounded hand with the other hand. The other Turks slashed at the boys until they went down, beaten.

3

Avak was paralyzed and shivering with fright. He knew there was no escape. He kept hearing his mother's warning "Stay here, don't move and don't make a sound." He watched his father and brothers ready to die for her.

Avak slammed his fists into the ground, pounding and pounding until they were raw. His father lunged again at the attackers but this time the saber came down on his head. There was no movement. Nothing! His brothers were wounded and not able to fight them off. They moaned and tried to reach their mother. One violent soldier approached each boy, pulled his hair, bringing his head back then slitting his throat.

Avak, stunned at the sight of the blood gushing from his brother's throats kept from passing out by staring at his mother, the urine running down his leg. She was unconscious on the ground. The captain walked over to Agavni and slapped her face. When she groaned he could see her eyes flutter open. He lifted his sword high in the air with both hands and when her eyes opened wide he stabbed her through the chest so she would know that it was a Turk who killed her.

Avak, drooling, unknowingly and unconsciously whimpering, tried to bury his head.

"Did you hear anything?" says the captain. "Shush, be quiet! I think I heard something. Go back into the house and see if anyone is left." Then the captain surveyed the dead bodies with a gruesome smile slowly crossing his face.

4

The three soldiers obeyed. After a quick search they came back, shook their heads.

"There's no one in the house. Come on let's get out of here."

"Are you sure no one is in the house?" questioned the captain.

"No one's in the house. We got 'em all. We did what we came here to do.

Now let's get the hell outta here and get the Armenian blood off of us."

With their slaughter behind them, they mounted their horses and rode off, the horses' hooves kicking dust into the air. Avak lay comatose under the porch, his mind and body in shock. Just as he thought they were gone, one came back and threw a flaming torch at the house and rode away into the night.

Avak knew he had to get out from under the porch before the flames reached him, but his body wouldn't move. The smoke was choking him and burning his eyes. Only through sheer will of survival did he crawl to his dead, bloodied family.

Eyes filled with tears, he picked up his mother's bed clothes and covered her naked body, gently, trying to avoid her dark, lifeless eyes. His vision was so blurred he couldn't see the carnage clearly, just blood, blood everywhere. He tried to speak but no words would form as his heart cried,

"Mommy, Daddy, Nazor, Arshag, what shall I do? Where should I go? What's to become of me? How am I going to live without you?" In abject despair he collapsed in their blood next to them.

CHAPTER 1

Ansonia, Connecticut May 23, 1911

Lukas Mollis was anticipating a big day. Preparing to fetch his family from Ellis Island on the following day, he was excited, but he didn't feel well. A persistent pain on his right side had him concerned. After having a light supper in his small room in the rooming house he managed, he went to bed early. Becoming restless during the night he tried to ignore the gnawing pain. In a stupor he groggily got up and walked across the wooden floor to the free standing sink. Taking some paregoric the doctor had given him made him feel as though the pain should subside. When he awoke in the early morning the pain was still there, but seemed more sporadic.

He had been waiting for this day for weeks. He made sure all was in place for his family's arrival. Extra beds were set up and more blankets were stored in closets along with pillows, pillow cases and towels. Ample food was in the small ice box. His boss was so kind to assist him in every way he could. Lukas' boss, Adreas, was the manager of this twenty unit rooming house that Lukas kept tidy and presentable. Once his family arrived, they would have to make arrangements to live elsewhere. This rooming house was only for single men.

"Well, Lukas, is everything ready for the big day?"

"Yes, yes. I can't wait to see my family. It's been two years since my boys and I left Eressos. How my children must have grown. Thank you for helping me prepare for them."

"If you need anything more, just ask. The best of luck to you and your family; I look forward to meeting them." He waved backhandedly while walking away as his voice trailed off.

"Thank you, Andreas. Thank you." Lukas shouted back.

He waited anxiously for his cousin, Andrew, to pick him up. He began to break out in a sweat and he thought, 'I must just be nervous.' When Andrew arrived, he took one look at him and said,

"What's wrong with you? You look terrible."

"I don't know I've had this pain on my side." Then he doubled over and was soaked with perspiration.

"I'm taking you right to the hospital."

"No, you can't. I have to pick up the family."

"Let's just check you out, okay?"

"Okay." He agreed reluctantly.

Andrew drove as fast as he could in his new Model T and pulled up to the hospital where aides helped him get Lukas into the Emergency Room. The doctor, in his long white coat, took him immediately into an examining room. Within minutes he came to Andrew and said Lukas needed emergency surgery.

"But his family from Greece is waiting for him at Ellis Island."

"Yes, he explained that to me. We'll take care of him and you bring his family here without delay. He is very sick."

"Please tell him I went to bring his family home."

CHAPTER 2

Virginia Mollis – Arriving in America

Ellis Island – May 23, 1911

Her arduous journey was coming to an end. At ten years old, Virginia couldn't remember how many days they had been on the ship, but it was more than a week. Steerage class was relegated to the bottom of the liner where the turbulence was more intense when the seas raged. No one escaped sea sickness. Virginia worried that the stench of vomit would never leave her nostrils and wondered if she would ever see sun light. But, finally, the day had arrived when this agony would end.

Her soiled, stained dress, that was so nice when she left Eressos, just hung on her. She couldn't remember the last time she ate anything more than hard bread. Her shoes were small when she put them on before the trip, but now her feet hurt all over. As the ship slowly entered

Manhattan, excitement began to build. At this time, she and her confined passengers were now allowed on deck. Someone yelled, "There she is, there she is," pointing and waving his hands. Her mom lifted her up to see the Statue of Liberty. Then she lifted her older sister, Dorothy, as well. Virginia grabbed Dorothy, and hugged her tight!

"We're here! We're going to see daddy!"

Virginia was so relieved. She anticipated this exciting moment, but wished she had the strength to run about the deck, now that it was permitted.

"We're here! We're finally here."

Virginia twirled around until she got dizzy. She was happy for two reasons. One was she felt as if she had been punished, living in a dungeon, and now she was freed. Secondly, she and her family would be with her daddy. He had come here first with her three brothers two years before to become established, and then he sent for them.

The steamship pulled into harbor with carnival fanfare. Horns blared announcing their arrival as the passengers eagerly lined up, enjoying the welcome. Virginia thought the gulls were even welcoming them! She kept trying to jump up to see over the heads of people in front of her, to catch a glimpse of her daddy.

"I can't wait to see daddy." She squealed to her sister, jumping up and down, envisioning his cheery face when he saw her. "I wish Theresa could be here with us, but maybe she'll come soon when her rash clears up."

Virginia's thoughts went to Theresa as she imagined her, living with Aunt Chrisanthe. She isn't really their aunt, but they call her aunt. Everyone knew she was obsessed with her son, so Theresa wouldn't be treated as well as she would have with someone else. But, her mother had no choice. Theresa was rejected at the point of entry and Chrisanthe was right there, offering to take her. Little did we know what Aunt Chrisanthe would do to her.

Theresa is only six and, Virginia was confident that her daddy would find a way to bring her to America very soon. She remembered Theresa's face when she gave her cloth spin doll to her to stop her from crying.

When they left Theresa behind, her mother, Cynthia, cried during the whole trip.

When the children asked her to stop crying, she would say,

"You children are like my fingers. They are all different, but they belong to my hand. When one of my fingers hurts, my whole hand hurts. When one of my children hurt, all of me hurts."

Virginia prayed that Theresa would come soon so her mother would stop hurting, and vowed to do whatever it took to ease her mother's pain.

The metal gang plank hit the ground with a crack of thunder. The girls jumped. They watched as the first- class passengers disembarked from the ship; they were allowed off first. They were dressed so nicely, leaving Virginia and Dorothy ashamed of their rags in comparison.

Throngs of people gathered on the docks and cheered the arrivals. There was excitement in the air, but the girls were too hungry and weak to care, and it seemed to make their mother more nervous.

The passengers in steerage had to wait for the ferry that would take them to Ellis Island where they were to be processed. Standing in line Virginia noticed the elevated trains and various venders beckoning customers. 'Maybe daddy's on that train.' They boarded the undersized ferry and took the short ride. But now this trip became more laborious. They were tired and the ferry was so crowded they could barely move.

When they left the ferry they had to stand in line again. Some women, dressed in grey uniforms, gave sandwiches and milk to them. They were so ravenous they devoured them immediately. It seemed to perk them up a bit.

After walking through the large metal doors, they looked around them and marveled at the size of the building.

They had never been in such a big room with giant windows. This, too, was overwhelming.

Every sound seemed to be magnified, making the girls feel as though this America was bigger than anything they had ever imagined.

Everyone was talking loudly in different languages. Each had a number from the manifesto, pinned on them. They followed the crowd up the stairs as their names were called. Tattered suitcases and ragged bundles in tow, they were part of the crowd.

"Maybe someone knows where daddy is. I really thought he would be waiting for us."

"Me, too."

Holding hands they stayed close to their mother.

A woman in a brown dress and matching hat led the group. She spoke in different languages so each person could understand her instructions.

"If you are waiting for someone to come for you, please have a seat in this room."

Loud conversations and children's cries were leaping off the walls. As their names were called, each had a physical exam. When it was Virginia's turn to be examined the doctor asked, through an interpreter,

"What's this sac pinned to your undershirt?"

She answered with pride pointing to the sac, "That's a piece of garlic my mother puts on us to ward off sickness, especially while we were on the ship." He just nodded and responded with a "humph" and a crooked smile. She gave him a big smile, proud of her mom. She stood patiently, optimistically waiting, while rocking on her heels, as her mom and sister completed their exams.

Once that was over they went back to the benches to wait. They watched as families came to meet their loved ones, hugged and kissed, leaving so happy. Virginia felt such a longing. 'Please, daddy, please come and get us.' Now they were becoming restless. They each wanted to sit next to their mother but there was very little room. Their mother had to reprimand them. This was something they rarely did, but they were so disoriented and fatigued.

Suddenly they were all alone and daddy hadn't shown. Virginia felt a rumbling in her stomach. She didn't know if it was from indigestion from eating too fast and going so long with nothing in her stomach, or just fear that he wasn't coming. They stopped pestering their mother as anticipation turned to dread.

Soon Virginia couldn't hold back her tears. Where could he be? I have so much to tell him. I want to tell him how much I missed him and how much I missed the way he twirled me in the air. She needed to confess something to him, too, that had been gnawing at her heart since he left them. She'd been rehearsing how she would tell him.

'Daddy, I have to tell you something. When it was my turn to feed the donkey, Kula, I thought I

would save time by giving him one feeding instead
of three. Well, he ate too much and when I went to
see him he had died. Mommy got upset because
she gets tired walking, and when she rode Kula,
she didn't get so tired.' She wondered if he would
get upset with her too for what she had done. She
wondered whether dad would kill her on this
confession, but she was prepared to die. She
wanted to be the one to tell him.

Trying to stifle her tears she looked over at her
mom and could see the anxiety on her face as she
knotted her fingers and rocked back and forth.

Suddenly, at the large entrance to the room,
they saw Andrew, their mother's cousin, calling,

"Cynthia, Cynthia"

Cynthia turned and saw Andrew standing there
waving.

Astounded, she blurted, "What are you doing
here? Where's Lukas?"

The girls screamed with anticipation, "Where's
daddy?" getting up from their seats, searching for
him, thinking he was coming up the stairs.

"He didn't feel well so I came to get you and the
children." He answered with his eyes downcast,
avoiding a direct look into their eyes.

"He didn't feel well? No, no. There's something
wrong. He should be here. You're not telling me
everything. Where is he? Where is he?"

She walked over to Andrew and held him by his lapels.

"Tell me the truth. Where is he? There has to be something terribly wrong for him not to be here." Shaking and trembling; her eyes filled with tears and she almost collapsed.

"He became very sick when I went to get him and I took him to the hospital immediately. He's having an operation. I'm going to bring you and the children to him right away. Don't worry. He'll be okay. We'll talk on the train. Right now let's concentrate on getting the ferry. Come on, kids." he encouraged, kissing each of them as they made their way.

"He's having an operation? How could this happen? What are we to do? How long is it going to take to get to the hospital? We have to take a train? Oh God, I have to see him. Please, please, hurry, hurry. He must be so very sick."

They had to line up again at the dock to board the ferry to Staten Island, Cynthia, sporadically bursting into tears. On board, it was overcrowded and smelly. None of the occupants had bathed, so the stench was overpowering. The motor strained, frightening the passengers. Virginia felt sick and a sense of emptiness. She too, like her mother, felt something was very wrong. She vomited bile all over her dress. There was something desperate about this turn of events. Even the slap of the agitated water around the hull of the ship gave her an eerie and unsettled feeling.

Virginia turned to her sister, "If daddy couldn't come, why didn't the boys come?"

"I don't know, but daddy's very sick." And she began to cry unable to catch her breath.

Andrew, trying to stop them from crying, pointed to the Statue of Liberty and her significance, and the majestic New York sky line, but the girls were not interested. Their thoughts were of their dad and of how sick he must be.

Getting off the ferry and waiting for the train had an altogether different aura than when they got off the steamer. Virginia thought, 'Daddy must be very sick. You don't go to the hospital unless you are very sick. She closed her eyes and said a silent prayer to God to make daddy better. Instead of anticipation and excitement, she felt foreboding and apprehension.

While boarding the train, Virginia looked up at the bellowing trail of smoke, bruising the picture perfect midnight blue sky. It was the first train ride they ever had. Living in their small village of Eressos, Greece, they never even saw a train. Watching the conductor swinging a lantern and shouting, "All aboard, all aboard" the girls hung on to each other, then a loud whistle. The train started to chug along, first very slowly then it began to pick up speed. Virginia's stomach leaped as she smelled the smoke from burning coal. Now she leaned back in her seat and thought, 'Where's daddy, where are my brothers? Theresa is still in Eressos. What's happening to my family?'

Cynthia looked at Andrew and asked, "Why didn't the boys come? Where are John, Tom and Charlie?"

"They are mining in Alaska."

Stunned, she screeched, "Mining in Alaska? Why?"

"They went to make some fast money. They should be back soon."

"Now they had to go? Tell me, did the doctor say what was wrong with Lukas?"

"He has what they call appendicitis. I left him in very good hands."

The train ride seemed long and tedious. The children slept on and off. Arriving in the New Haven station it was much smaller than Grand Central in New York, but the same brick buildings, paved roads and trolley cars. They walked to Andrew's car waiting in the parking lot and headed for Saint Raphael's Hospital. Andrew had some fruit and crackers for them in the car and handed them out. The car was very small, but the sisters sat in back and mother in front. No one spoke. Such a turn of events, who could have expected this?

When they arrived at the hospital, they looked around and saw patients groaning, some were bleeding; it were dirty, disgusting and smelly. Virginia felt sick and frightened. A nurse approached them and Andrew explained who they were. She escorted them down the white tiled hall way. Virginia couldn't take her eyes off the sick people in the emergency room as she followed, holding her mother's hand. It smelled of ether, sickness and death all the way to the conference room.

"The doctor will be here momentarily."

"It smells funny in here." Virginia nudged Dorothy.

"I know. "It's making me sick. I have a bitter taste in my mouth."

The doctor, dressed in a long white coat, his glasses resting at the tip on his nose, came in and closed the door. He introduced himself, while avoiding their gaze, proceeded to tell them the most horrific news they could imagine.

"We were unable to save your husband. He died two hours after surgery."

"What did he say?" Cynthia questioned Andrew.

Andrew told her and the children in Greek, "Lukas has passed away."

She began to scream, clutching at her chest. The children buried their head in their hands whispering softly, "No, no, no."

"He died? He died? This can't be happening." Howled Cynthia, wide eyed and trembling. She collapses on the dirty floor, the children engulfed her.

"No," cried Dorothy, struggling to hold on to someone or something.

The nurse came in and brought them water and stroked their heads, and tried to console them, but it was futile. Other nurses came into the room and tried to comfort them. They didn't understand English so their words were empty. However, their touch and embraces were, to some extent, comforting.

"Come, Cynthia, I'm going to take you and the children to my house."

"I want to see him. Please let me see him." She screamed, begging pathetically, as she wrung her handkerchief, asking for an interpretation.

The doctor led the way as Andrew took her arm. The children held hands firmly as they followed down a long, dimly lit, white tiled corridor, their heads bowed. They walked into an all white room. A lone stretcher covered with a wrinkled white sheet was in the center of the room. The attendant pulled the sheet from the stretcher and they saw their father's face, eyes closed and peaceful.

"Husband, my husband, what's going to happen to us? How could you die? I waited so long to be with you. Why? Why? We were going to be together and never be apart. That's what you said, remember? Don't you remember? You promised me. You promised." Whispering now as her face was drenched in her tears and saliva, Cynthia threw herself over him and wept and kissed him until Andrew struggled to pull her off of him. She wouldn't let go.

Cynthia put her hand to his face and wailed. The children held on to their mother and cried with her, trying to bury their faces in her skirt. Andrew had to pry them away after what seemed much too long.

Andrew started walking them out the door when Virginia yelled, "I don't want to leave. I want to stay here with daddy. Maybe they made a mistake. Maybe he'll wake up. No, no, I can't leave," pulling away from them. Dorothy knew better, being the older sister. She took her hand and helped Andrew get them to leave the room.

Andrew held all of them close to him as they were escorted from the room. He led them down the hallway, down the steps and to his car as a slight drizzle began. The wind had picked up now and blew in bursts of fury, the air turned frightfully chilly.

"This is the worst day of my life." cried Virginia, "My poor daddy." We weren't here to comfort him and hold his hand. He was here all alone. He was alone. What's going to happen to us? What's going to happen?"

They were numb, like being suspended in air. Andrew tried to reassure them on the way home. "I'll take care of you. I'll take care of you."

But their whole world had just split open and they were spiraling down into a deep dark hole.

The funeral was the next day. The church service was held at Holy Trinity Church. Lukas' boss, Mr. Andreas, came. Some of the tenants from the boarding house came as well. The girls and their mother didn't know them, but it was nice that they came. The Pine Grove Cemetery was adjacent to the church. The pall bearers were provided by the funeral home. Virginia, Dorothy and Cynthia followed the priest and the coffin to the burial site, clinging to their mother.

The priest read some more prayers. It was drizzly and the ground was sopping wet, but they didn't seem to notice. The cemetery attendants placed two ropes underneath the casket and slid it over the crypt. Very slowly they lowered the casket into the ground. Cynthia began to wail, grabbing at her chest, ripping at her dress. This was the finale, the end! Andrew grabbed her before she threw herself into the grave. "Cynthia, stop!" He embraced her, stroking her. "Come, it's time to go." Andrew's wife, Angie, held on to the girls, brushing back their hair. "Come, come, it's time to go."

They went to Lukas' apartment and packed his meager belongings, then headed to Andrews' house in Middletown. On the way, he and Angie explained that they owned a three family house and Cynthia and the children could live on the second floor. It's furnished and ready to move in. The boys will come soon and you'll feel much better. You'll see.

Virginia thought, 'There's no way we will ever feel better.'

CHAPTER 3

Virginia in the United States

Summer turned into fall, fall into winter and winter back to spring. Reality was setting in for Virginia and for Avak in two different parts of the world. Virginia was adjusting to American life without her father, and Avak was suffering through the loss of his whole family while living with his uncle in Marseille, France.

Her three brothers returned from Alaska. Charles and Tom left after a few days for California. John stayed with his mother and the girls, but this wasn't out of kindness.

In the sparsely furnished bedroom Virginia shared with her sister, she cried herself to sleep more often than not. Her pillow awash with tears, she turned to her in the twin bed next to her.

"Dorothy, I can't sleep. Are you awake?"

"No, I'm not sleeping and I'm not crying either. Why are you crying?" she snapped, agitated.

"I don't want to be here. I miss Theresa."

"I miss Theresa, too, and I don't want to be here either, but we have no choice."

"I don't want to be here without daddy. Everyone in my class has a daddy. Why couldn't they save him?" She sobbed, tears spilling over her colorless cheeks.

"You know, I've been thinking." Dorothy started to say as she moved over into her sister's bed. "If daddy had appendicitis in Eressos, he would have died before they could even get him to the hospital. We can't question these things, as mommy says."

"I know if I think the way you just said, you're right. But I had so many plans. He was going to show us America. Now, we're in Andrew's house, go to school and come home. I don't have any friends and the kids make fun of my English." Tears were still flooding the pillow.

"The kids make fun of me, too. But I don't pay attention. You shouldn't either. Soon we'll speak just like they do, you'll see. It takes time. Now go to sleep and dream good thoughts."

Dorothy went back to her bed. Virginia thought, 'She wants me to dream good thoughts but I can't think of any.' She looked at the vine covered wallpaper and noticed it peeling away from the wall close to the ceiling. This is like my life, just peeling away.'

CHAPTER 4

Marseille, France
Avak Achjian – aka – George Avak

In Marseille, France, Avak was scared and lonely.

"I don't want to go to school." He whined, shaking his head.

"You should go to school. You will make some friends," his uncle urged.

"We must be grateful to the French for giving us refugees a place to live and for you young ones to go to school. Come on, we'll go together. It's been a long time since you've had any schooling."

He rubbed Avak's shoulders, giving him encouragement, while helping him up. Reluctantly Avak walked with him, not wanting to go to school.

He thought to himself, 'There's no point in going to school because there's no point in living.'

Proceeding across the muddy, pebbled ground, Avak could smell the familiar intoxicating aromas of roasted lamb with herb spices from back home. It made him even more homesick and brought back memories of that fateful day. When they entered the classroom, kids of all ages were sitting at make-shift desks set on the ground with a tent for a roof. The teacher was an Armenian priest just like Avak's uncle. Both were imposing figures in black suits and dark, trimmed beards with speckles of grey.

"Come, come." The instructor beckoned, smiling and motioning with his hand. "Come, sit. You must be Avak. I've heard so much about you. Hello Father Devletian."

The two men shook hands as Avak slid into an uneven seat, unwillingly. His uncle whispered. "I'll be back to get you. You'll be fine."

"I'm Father Tobian but everybody calls me Father T. Allow me to introduce you to everyone. He said each person's name and Avak counted twelve kids of all ages.

Avak looked slightly different from the others. They all had dark hair and dark eyes. However, his eyes were almond shaped with curly lashes, almost girlish, and his hair was thick, curly and unruly. He had a pronounced cleft in his substantial chin and he was very tall for his age. He was strikingly handsome, with a chiseled face, and his

29

complexion was fairer than most. The space in between his two front teeth, inherited from his father, made him feel special and unique.

'Every kid here must have suffered in some way at the hands of the Turks.' Avak thought. He still felt alone even though his uncle was kind, and introduced him to new people. He wondered if these kids had a mother and father, and if they had siblings. He couldn't help but feel that God had singled him out to suffer so greatly.

At the end of the lesson Avak sat waiting for his uncle to come. Father T. came and sat next to him and waited, too. He put his arm around Avak and said, "Your mother is smiling that her brother has found you and will care for you. I'm so sorry for your suffering. All of us here have suffered irreparable losses at the hands of the Turks.

"What happened to you, Father?" he asked.

With a pained look on his face, he began his story. "I had a parish in Aleppo. During our Good Friday evening service the Turks surrounded us and set my church on fire. A few escaped, but most perished."

"Ugh!" Avak gasped, breathing in too much air, and gulped. "How did you ever escape?"

"A German soldier, who was assigned to this particular Turkish regiment, saw me trying desperately to escape. He grabbed me and rolled me in a carpet and took me out; pretending to be taking a carpet from the church. I waited until all was quiet and unrolled myself from the carpet to find myself alone with no Turks around me and my church burned to the ground. I thank God I was saved. But I never knew what became of the people of my parish. I don't know where they are. I don't know who survived. I do know that God was with me." Avak just shook his head, choking back tears. Then his uncle, Father Devletian came to get him. They said good-bye and Father T. said, "I'll see you tomorrow, Avak, yes?"

"Yes Father, "I'll see you tomorrow."

Walking back to their home Avak asked his uncle, "Why do you think the Turks singled out us Armenians to torture and kill?"

Father rubbed his chin, pondering the question: "I think, first we were Christians in a Muslim country and have always been treated badly. The "Young Turks" hate us. Murder, destruction and torture occupy the minds of the "Young Turks." When the deportations weren't fast enough, then the outright murders took place. The Armenian Tatar massacred families at random to create fear. Now they just enjoy it. They have killed Greeks and Albanians, too, all of them Christians. But none have suffered as much as we Armenians and I don't know all the reasons why. I just know they want to obliterate us from the earth."

This was too much for Avak to totally understand.

"Uncle, how can you be a priest and believe in God after what He has allowed the Turks to do to us?"

He put his arm around Avak and explained. "Son, it's not God's fault. God created people. He gave them a brain with the ability to think and act. What they do with it, is in their hands. If they don't follow the teachings of Christ, and they choose to commit torture and murder, they will perish in hell."

"You mean we have to wait for them to die for their punishment?"

"That's what we believe. It doesn't always work that way of course. If someone is accused of murder in the United States and other free countries around the world, they go to court, and if found guilty, they are punished."

"Then there is justice in other countries?"

"Yes there is justice, freedom, choices -- all those things in the United States. I am hoping to be assigned there and when I am, I will take you with me."

"America? You mean I could live in America?"

"Yes, not only you could, but you will."

Now he had something to latch on to. He had something to look forward to. That night was the first night he fell asleep without nightmares; maybe there's a place for me after all.

The next day he looked forward to school. He was still tempted to look over his shoulder but avoided the urge, walking purposefully. The sky was promising with a few shards of the sun peeking through the trees. He sat next to a boy who had the same name as his brother, Arshag. He leaned over to him and whispered,

"My brother's name was Arshag, too, but he died with my whole family.
They killed them all."

"You mean they killed your whole family?"

"Yes, my mother, my father and my two older brothers. I watched the slaughter. My mother hid me under the porch and then she went back into the house. She saved my life. If she had stayed with me, they would have come looking for her and found me too." As he said this, he realized this was the truth. He was saved. That was her last act of undying love.

"Oh my God, you saw the whole thing, you poor kid."

"Yes I did. I thought I was the only one who had suffered but I'm not alone. What happened to you?"

"My father was a doctor." Arshag said. He and several other doctors were being stalked by the Turks to be killed. They hung my father and twelve other doctors by their feet from a cliff. When they were almost dead they cut the rope and let them plunge into the ravine to their death." He said this as he stared into space, wide eyed and scarcely blinking. "I can't believe I'm telling you this; a total stranger."

Avak, eyes filled with tears, looked traumatized. He felt a sense of closeness to Arshag that he was willing to share this with him.

"Night time brings bad dreams and I wake in a soaking sweat. How do you get to sleep at night?" Avak asked, looking at him, with a smear of disbelief.

"I feel I'm luckier than most. My mother's friend smuggled us out and we landed here. I like school, and I want to be a doctor like my father."

"How did you get here?" Arshag asked.

"I don't remember anything. My uncle says that I came on a French ship with his name pinned on my shirt. He's my mother's brother and the only relative I have in the world, and I didn't even know him."

"What did your father do?"

"He had a store in the bazaar. He sold carpets. My two brothers worked with him. Maybe the Turks knew who they were and came after them or maybe it was just at random. I will never know. Sometimes I wake up in a cold sweat. I dream they are coming after me. Sometimes I find myself looking over my shoulder thinking they have found me and are going to kill me. I know I have to change my name."

Arshag whispered, "I've heard they march women and children in the blistering sun to a 'refugee camp'. They never make it because they starve them and beat them so they will die on the way. Some they rape and tie to a stake and ride their horses by them, as fast as they can, as they chop off their heads, while their children watch."

"Oh My God!" Avak whispered "It just gets worse and worse," shaking his head with his face buried in his hands, feeling nauseous.

After his talk with Arshag, he realized more and more how many of his nationality had suffered. Were the Turks possessed by the devil? Was their objective to totally wipe out the Armenian population? He would learn more horror stories during his stay in Marseille. With each story his heart broke, but now he had a friend who understood his plight, just like a brother.

One day Avak decided to take a different route home from school. Now that he had been here for four years, he felt more confident in his surroundings. Walking down a street that had shops, he could hear the whirling of a machine. Peeking around the corner he saw two men, each sitting at his sewing machine making what looked like men's clothing. He walked in and smiled.

"Hey, could you show me how to do that?"

"Sure. Come on in. Do you think you'd like to become a tailor?"

"I don't know. It looks like something I could do."

"Have a seat. I'll show you."

After his first lesson the two men asked him to come by after school. They would instruct him, and he could do some deliveries for them for a few francs.

"It sounds like a plan and thanks."

He learned how to thread the machine, thread the bobbin through the surface and loop it through behind the needle. He learned how to sew a straight line using the foot bar with both feet controlling the speed; back and forth, back and forth. As he learned more, the men seemed pleased with his progress.

Making a delivery one day, he passed a young girl sitting on the stoop near the road. She was facing downward tracing the cracks along the road with her forefinger. He noticed her hands seemed older than her years, her nails bitten to the quick and her hair disheveled, long, black and curly. When she looked up at him he saw paths of tear tracks along her cheeks.

"Are you okay?"

She shook her head, no.

"What's your name?"

"Elizabeth"

"Well, Elizabeth, I have to make a delivery just down the street. Would you like to walk with me?"

She got up and started to walk with him.

"You're Armenian, right?"

"Yes, I am."

"No matter how bad things are, you should know that all of us Armenians have suffered. You are not alone."

She stopped while looking at her hands and said, "No, my life is over and I'm only fifteen years old."

They walked along the cobblestone road searching for the right street. Avak noticed she kept her head down as she walked and avoided looking into his eyes. He delivered the suit, and they continued to walk. He felt so sorry for her and felt as though he had to do something to cheer her.

"You know there's a bazaar on Saturday. My friend, Arshag, and I are planning to go; would you like to come with us?" trying to be cheerful.

"No. I can't."

"Yes you can. My friend and I will pick you up at 10:00 right here, okay? It will be something different to do."

"No. I can't." as she kicked a stone with her foot.

"Look, it's just a bazaar. We'll see things we've never seen before. It will be an adventure."

"Oh, okay."

"Good. See you Saturday, Elizabeth."

He left her and was pleased with himself that he had convinced her to join them. He couldn't help but feel something terrible had happened to this girl. Her eyes were already dead.

Saturday was a magnificent day. The air was clear and the sun shone through cotton filled clouds dispersed ever so thinly in the sky. Arshag and Avak picked up Elizabeth and they walked about a half hour to the bazaar. Avak took in the spectacular architecture on the very wide streets. Flowers graced the buildings as though they had been strategically placed. Elizabeth was quiet, pensive and avoided their eyes. Arshag tried to make small talk but she was unreachable.

"Do you have family here?" he asked.

"No, I have no one, anywhere."

"Where are you from?"

"Smyrna." still avoiding eye contact.

"What happened to you in Smyrna?"

"I don't want to talk about it."

The boys knew they had to stop asking questions, so they did.

The bazaar was like nothing they had ever seen before. There were so many kinds of birds in cages. They were small and large and every color imaginable. Some cages had as many as fifty in them. Arshag said he wished he could have one but knew it was impractical.

"Nah" Avak said. "I think they're pretty but I wouldn't want one."

There were hundreds of carpets, men and woman's clothing, shoes, dishes and then they smelled chocolate. They ran to the candy cart.

"Elizabeth, when was the last time you had something chocolate?"

"I can't remember."

"I can't remember either."

The boys pooled their francs and bought a chocolate candy for each of them. Elizabeth ate hers, but she didn't have the reaction the boys hoped she would; however they savored every morsel. "Mm this is so good. I'm just going to let it melt in my mouth. I won't even chew it." said

Arshag. They moseyed through the bazaar some more until they got hungry. Walking back home Avak invited Elizabeth and Arshag for lunch but Arshag had to get home. Arshag went one way and Avak and Elizabeth went the other way. Agnes, the woman who cooked for the priests, made them some lunch and Avak told Elizabeth he would walk her home. He was disappointed his uncle wasn't home; he wanted his uncle to talk to her to see if he could help.

"Who are you staying with if you have no family?"

"Friends of my mother; I have no idea what's going to happen to me."

"Why don't you come to school with Arshag and me? You'll meet some new kids and your life will change."

"My life will never change. I can never change what happened to me."

They reached the stoop where he originally found her that day and they sat together.

"Please tell me what happened to you."

"Okay, I'll tell you," fidgeting with her fingers. "My father was a member of the underground against the Turks in Smyrna. There was increasing unrest between us and the Turks. To get even with my father, three Turks cornered me in my yard when I was twelve years old. My father came rushing out of the house trying to save me. But soldiers forced him back and made him watch as they tore off my clothes and raped me one by one. I was screaming, "Daddy, daddy, daddy." My father was yelling my name over and over; screaming with anguish. The last word I heard my father say was: – E-l-i-z-a-b-e-t-h. The Turks left me lying on the ground and killed my father before they torched my house. Then they came back and marked me as being raped so no one would ever want me. She lifted up her bangs and showed him a purplish green mark on her forehead. That's why I wear my hair over my forehead."

"And that's why you won't look at me?"

She nodded her head.

"But that wasn't your fault!"

She started to sob, then to weep uncontrollably as her body quivered.

"They should have killed me too. Why didn't they just kill me?" She buried her head in his shoulder and continued to cry.

He put his arms around her and his own trauma came into focus as he lamented with her. They stood embracing for a long while. Then she looked up at him and said,

"Why are you crying too?

"Because. You are breaking my heart. You can't feel your life is over. You have to go on. Don't you see? If you feel shame, they have won. You must go on and make a life. Then they are defeated."

He took her hand and tried to kiss her cheek but she pulled away and ran into the house.

She turned to him as she entered the doorway and said, "Good-bye."

That wasn't I'll see you soon. It was good-bye.

He had failed. He couldn't reach her. He could never reach her. There was nothing he could do for her, or for himself, for that matter except to leave here. How many more stories would he hear? How many more before he, himself, would be lost forever?

He looked down at his hand where there was a purplish green mark in between his thumb and his forefinger. He had noticed the mark when he got to Marseille. He had no recollection how it got there, but it was the same as Elizabeth's. What happened to him? Why was it there? Who did this to him?

Walking back home, he took a short cut. Lost in thought, he didn't realize that he was in a dark, narrow alley way with cobble stone streets. There were tall old brick buildings on either side. He had an eerie feeling, and began to run, wanting to get out of there. From one of the buildings several boys came rushing toward him.

"Give me your money." One said, speaking in French.

"I don't have any." Avak answered

"If you don't give us your money, we'll kill you."

Then they attacked him; swinging their fists into his face and throwing him to the ground and kicking him in the stomach. He was doubled over and a bloody mess. He thought. This is it. This is where I'm going to be killed. I will never see America. Then he heard a loud, strong voice, "Get away. Get away from that boy."

He looked up, and there was a huge man standing before him and then the boys scattered. The man picked him up and helped him into his apartment just across the way. He sat him on the couch and called for his wife.

"Monique, Monique, come quickly." She came into the room, sat next to him and put her arms around him. She said, "George, get some wet gauze and we'll clean his face. Oh you poor child."

"What's your name?"

"Avak Achjian."

"You have to be careful. It's dark and you can't walk these streets alone." George said, as he rushed back with the gauze.

"I guess I don't belong anywhere. I don't belong here either."

"What do you mean?"

"I am an Armenian refugee from Turkey where they kill Armenians. I came here and the French don't want me either."

"No, no. That's not true." George said.

"The boys who attacked you were gypsies, they were not Frenchmen. You are wanted here. These gypsies attack anyone for money, not just you."

Feeling Monique's arms around him, made him weep. It was the first time anyone had hugged him since his mother. The tears coming down his cheeks hurt and burned his raw skin. As she rocked him, he felt a sense of comfort. Oh how he missed his mother.

"You're all right Avak; you don't have any pain, do you?"

"No, no, just my face hurts and my stomach is sore."

"Here, have a little juice."

With her soft, cool hands she pushed away his hair from his face. He looked at them and he noticed her finger nails were painted bright red. He had never seen any woman with nail polish before. He looked into her eyes and thought he was looking at an angel. Not only was she a comfort to him, but she was beautiful. She was wearing a silk kimono with bright red flowers. Her hair was blonde piled up high. Her eyes were clear blue and she smelled of heavenly perfume; he was spellbound and he wanted to stay in her arms forever.

"My poor boy, my poor boy." She kept repeating.

It was getting late and George said he would walk him home. Avak, reluctantly left her arms and said good-bye to Monique and thanked her for being so kind. He wished he didn't have to leave. She took his face in her hands and kissed both cheeks. Oh how he didn't want to leave.

"How can I ever thank you for saving my life and for being so good to me? Avak posed looking straight into their friendly faces.

"You don't have to thank us." George said, holding on to Avak , helping him walk out the door.

"They would have killed me and no one would have known or cared."

"You have your whole life ahead of you, Avak. This is just an isolated incident that happens daily. Just put it out of your mind and watch where you walk from now on."

They reached his home and Father Devletian came rushing out.

"Where have you been, what happened? Oh my God look at you. Come in, come in."

George told him what had happened and Father thanked him, over and over, for saving Avak.

"Please sit with us and have something to eat."

"No, no, I have to get home, but Avak could use something to eat, right?"

"Yes, well, I am hungry."

"Okay, Avak, you're in good hands now. Just be careful." He hugged him and left.

"I owe that man my life and I will probably never see him again."

"I'm sure you'll find a way to remember him." Father said.

A few days later while making his deliveries, Avak made a little detour to visit Elizabeth. He knocked on her door and she answered without a smile.

"Hi, Elizabeth, how are you?"

"I'm okay."

"Would you like to take a walk with me? It's a beautiful day."

"Oh, okay." She said shrugging her shoulders.

She came outside and Avak couldn't help but notice she looked even paler and thinner than before.

"How are you feeling, Elizabeth?"

"I'm feeling fine, thank you."

"Have you given any more thought to coming to school and making new friends?"

"Yes, I have given it some thought."

"And what have you decided?"

"I have decided that I will not come to school."

"Can you give me a reason?"

"As I have told you before, there isn't a place for me in school. I don't want to be with people. I don't want to make friends." Her eyes were still focused on the ground.

"Okay, how about if I bring you to school. You won't be alone. I'll be with you."

"You mean you'll come and get me?"

"Yes, I'll come and get you."

"Okay, then I'll come, just this one time."

"I'll be here tomorrow at 8:00 sharp."

He took her hand in his and held it for a long while. She pulled away and ran back to her house. The next morning he got up early and looked forward to meeting her. He was so pleased with himself that he had convinced her to make this move. He knocked on the door and she opened it, standing there tense and scared.

Avak took a deep breath and said,

"Come on let's go." He put his hand out to grab hers and walk together, but she pulled away. That's okay he thought; can't expect too much on her first day.

Walking to school he pointed out where his friends lived and anything that would be of interest to her. When they got to school, Arshag was already there and got up to greet her. The boys stood on either side of her making the introductions. Fr. T. made room for her to sit in between them.

Avak could see she was way behind in school work for her age. He didn't want to make her feel uncomfortable by offering to tutor her, but in time he would. He was also surprised that she didn't know any of the students; they all lived within close proximity. Ah yes, he thought, she never leaves her yard. That's why she doesn't know anyone.

The class ended and Avak had to go to the tailor shop to get some deliveries.

"Elizabeth, I have to go to the tailor shop do you want to come with me?"

"Okay. Then you can walk me home."

"Of course, how did you like your first day of school?"

"It's okay."

They walked silently for a while then he began to tell her about some of the children in the classroom and the things they had all been through. He thought this might make her feel as though she wasn't alone in her suffering and be more amenable to being with people. She just listened without any response.

"I'm really tired," she said. "Do you mind if I go home?"

"No. Not if you're really tired."

He dropped her off before making his delivery and said, "See you in the morning."

"Okay."

He had a funny feeling that this wasn't going to work out. She wasn't interested. What more could he do? When he got home, he told Father what had transpired during the day.

"Well, son, you have done all you can do. See what happens tomorrow."

When tomorrow came, he got up early and went to pick her up. She answered the door and said she didn't feel well and couldn't go today.

"Are you okay? Do you need a doctor?"

"No, I just don't feel well today."

"Okay. Feel better. We'll miss you today."

She closed the door. Avak left her and knew this was just an excuse. He had failed again. He was falling for her but realized her suffering would never leave her, no matter how much he tried. Maybe he'd better leave her alone for her sake as well as his.

CHAPTER 5

Dreams Become Reality

As Father Devletian had anticipated, his transfer came through.

"Ah ha, Avak, we're going to the America." Father Devletian said, waving a letter and hurrying toward him.

"Finally your transfer came through?" His expression filled with excitement, his eyes widening.

"Yes, we're on our way to New York."

"What do I have to do? Tell me."

"I will take care of everything. You just tell your friends at school and the tailor shop that you are going to America."

This was his wish. He wanted to leave Marseille and start a new life. America was all the boys in his class talked about. Someday, someday, we'll go to America. His someday was here; it was now. He had another reason not to sleep at night, but this was for a good reason.

The day before they were to leave, Avak wanted to say good-bye to Elizabeth. He went to her home and knocked on the door. It took a long time for someone to answer. Finally, the door opened just a crack and a woman appeared in between the door jamb and the door, leaving just enough of an opening to expose a portion of her face.

"Is Elizabeth here?"

The woman shook her head, "No."

"Can I wait for her?"

"She's gone."

"She's gone where?"

"I have no idea. She ran away a week ago, and no one has seen or heard from her."

"Oh, My God."

"We did everything we could to try to help her, but she just couldn't overcome the shame that she felt."

"I could see it in her eyes. I knew she was defeated and beaten."

The woman opened the door wider now that she felt more comfortable. The house inside was nice and neat, smelling of Armenian cooking spices – just like home.

"My uncle is taking me to New York to live. Can I have your name so I can write to you? Maybe she'll come back. Can you tell her I was here? My name is Avak Achjian. She may have told you. We went to the bazaar together."

"Yes, of course, of course." She invited him in and wrote her name on a piece of paper. Every day I pray for her return, but as each day passes I lose hope."

"Thank you. Let's pray she returns safely."

"Yes, yes. Pray God."

He said good-bye to his friend Arshag and promised to meet up in New York. He said his good-byes to his tailor friends, and thanked them for teaching him valuable skills and for a letter of introduction to their friend in New York.

This time his voyage would be memorable. He was a young adult and he was going to America. Their accommodations were second class, not in steerage, so they received decent meals, primarily stews. They took in some fresh air on deck as weather permitted. Even though the trip was long, there were discussions with the men aboard about the opportunities in the United States and rewards for hard work.

When Avak left Marseille there were 80,000 Armenians there. They had settled in Lyon and Nice as well. These cities were beginning to build churches and schools and were developing into communities.

One afternoon while sitting on deck, Avak turned to Father Devletian and confessed,

"Of all the people I have met, the Armenian girls are very sad. I feel if I continue to associate with them they are just going to bring me down even more than I am."

"I understand the way you feel. However, in New York you are going to meet many people from all walks of life. My son, your life is just beginning and we are headed for the greatest hope in the world where dreams come true – The United States."

Avak parted with his uncle and promised to be in touch. They didn't want to say good-bye, and he didn't want to cry. They just hugged, saying so long, not a good-bye.

"You have my address at the Archdiocese, right?"

"Yes I do."

"Come and see me when you get settled; we'll do a little exploring together."

He took from his pocket the address that the tailors had given him and proceeded to walk on 7th Avenue. 'New York is easy', he thought. 'You just have to know how to count' as he tried to avoid horse droppings, mesmerized by the skyscrapers at the same time. He found the address and walked up two flights of stairs, suitcase in hand. He knocked on the door and when someone called, "Come in." He opened the door. There stood a man who looked just like his father, and Avak gasped.

"Ah, hello, I'm Avak Achjian; are you Mr. Kormanian?"

"Yes I am. Mashallah!" He exclaimed, getting up from his chair and opening his arms to him. "Welcome, Welcome. Just call me Jake. I've been expecting you and here you are. I hear you're a very good tailor. I have a friend who is looking for tailors. But first let's have some coffee and you can tell me about your trip and I'll tell you about New York; come sit, sit."

They visited for a while and Jake told him about the ins and outs of New York and how people come to New York to escape their troubled lives. "Be careful. Someone is always looking to take advantage of young immigrants."

As they walked to the next building Avak felt queasy. He kept stealing glimpses of Jake while thinking of his father. Of course he got the job, working long hours for short pay. He found a rental in a tenement building on 8th Avenue. He worked on 7th Avenue so he could walk to work. The factory was located on the top floor of the building. Sewing machines took up the whole floor from front to back. After the fire of 1900, employees were no longer locked in the factory and were allowed bathroom breaks. Those conditions never returned. During that fire the employees couldn't escape and over 800 people perished.

The conditions were still poor, but Avak learned how to make men's and woman's suits; and women's dresses. The company was owned by two Jewish men who were strict and frugal. It was required that each employee be responsible for purchasing his own thread and needles. Working from 7:00 AM to 6:00 PM Avak saved his money, opened a bank account and took in all the sights that were free.

The factory was referred to as a sweat shop. In the summer, the fourth floor, where he worked, became so hot even the two large fans in the rear of the room didn't give much relief. They were paid by the piece. One week he worked on lapels, with muslin facing, and the next week it was sleeves.

The less experienced tailors worked next to more experienced ones. The supervisors would patrol the aisles, make corrections or instruct them to start over. Every time you made a mistake, it cost you money. The more pieces you could complete in a day, the more money you made.

Avak was so tired by the end of the day, there was nothing left to do but get something to eat and go to bed. Most of the sewers were immigrants.

Most of them did not speak English, so he didn't make any friends. However, one day, rolling down his shirt sleeve with his jacket slung over his shoulder, he was approached by a fellow about his age.

"Hi, my name is Tony Mascarelli. What's yours?"

"I'm Avak Achjian," extending his hand. "It's good to meet you."

It was clear from that moment they would become friends. They would take walks and talk about their future, knowing full well this couldn't be all there was to life.

Avak often walked down to the pier, alone, and looked at the Statue of Liberty and Ellis Island off in the distance. He marveled at the tug boats guiding the tankers into the harbor. He would get an ice cream and think how lucky he was to be here. Even though life was difficult and lonely, he was free and becoming less afraid. His life belonged to him. He liked his new Italian friends who were tailors as well. Having some friends relieved some of the loneliness he felt and the sense that if he died no one would ever know or care.

"Hey, Avak, I'll take a walk with you down to the pier."

"Sure come on, Tony."

They spoke of the day they arrived and how fortunate they were to find work and a place to live;

and of course living in the renowned New York City.

"Do you want to learn how to dance?"

"I know how to Armenian dance."

"No, I mean ballroom dance."

"What's that?"

"Foxtrot, waltz, you know dance while holding a girl in your arms."

"Really?"

"Yeah, Saturday night on the lower west side of 5th. There's a night club there and it's '10 cents a dance.' What do you say we go?"

"It sounds good to me."

"I'll be by your apartment around 8:00."

"Good"

Saturday night came and Tony was waiting for Avak at 8:00, with hair combed, freshly pressed shirts and polished shoes they walked up 5th and down 27th. Admission was free, but if you wanted to dance you had to buy a ticket for 10 cents.

"Come on, Avak, let's get two tickets each and see how it goes."

"Okay," he shrugged, "We can only lose 20 cents."

The ballroom smelled of stale cigarettes. There was a mirrored ball hanging from the ceiling in the middle of the dance floor reflecting the lights as it rotated slowly. The men were in a circle clinging to the walls of the building. Some had been there before and some were awkward, just like Avak. The girls sauntered across the dance floor sizing up the men. Avak felt uneasy.

Avak perused the scene, and his eyes fell upon a sexy blue eyed blonde with long curly hair. She was wearing a flouncy, garish print dress of multicolored flowers. Her shoulders and arms were bare, exposing her flawless skin. She smiled as she placed herself in front of him. She put out her hand for the ticket and automatically Avak gave it to her, mesmerized. She took him by the hand and led him to the center of the dance floor. They settled into a dance position as the music played a foxtrot. She whispered in his ear, "One, two, three, four; one, two, three, four." Soon they were whirling around the floor as if Avak had danced all his life. He gave her a second ticket as a waltz started and they danced the waltz. When the dance was over she whispered to him,

"I could lose my job if I leave with you, so do you want to meet me outside at 10:00 when I get off?"

"Sure."

He went over to Tony and told him he had a date at 10:00.

"Okay" Tony said. "But be careful. These girls are shrewd."

Tony left and Avak waited. He paced back and forth becoming weary as time passed. 'Maybe I should just go home' he thought. But eventually she did come out and gave him her million dollar smile and took his arm. They walked on 5th and down to 6th. He liked the sound of her tapping high heels against the pavement. He was excited that she chose him for her date.

"So, what's your name?"

"Flo, what's yours?"

"Avak."

"That's a funny name."

"I know. I'm Armenian."

"What's Armenian?"

"Forget it." Right then he knew he had to change his name. Not only to hide from the Turks, but to avoid scenes like this.

They arrived at her tenement building and when she opened the door there were stairs directly in front of them, maybe around fourteen. He looked at the dimly lit hallway with chipped and gnarled walls of putrid yellow. He began to feel sick. They walked up the stairs to the landing and turned to another flight of stairs. Now Avak thought, 'what the hell is going on? What a dump.' She stopped in front of a door with the number 36 hand painted in black and unlocked it.

"This is it." She said turning to him and smiling. "Come on in as she closed the door behind them.

It was one room with only a floor lamp for light. A torn, stained shade tried unsuccessfully to cover a filthy window. An unmade large bed took up the whole room. It smelled like perfume was doused to cover up a putrid odor. She placed her pocketbook on her small dresser and proceeded to remove her clothes; first her dress and then her shoes. She removed his shirt, threw him on the bed and removed his shoes and pants. She got on top of him, kissed him on the mouth, all wet and gooey. She kept kissing him and rubbing her hands in places he knew she shouldn't. He felt a stirring inside of him and then she handed him something.

"Here put this on."

He was stunned and just did as he was told. They made love and he experienced a wild ecstasy. He was under her spell. She continually massaged his body from head to toe. In his delirium he fell into an unconscious sleep. When he awoke he was on the second landing, half dressed with his shoes on top of him.

"What the hell? What the hell's going on?"

He looked around. He was alone. He put on his shoes, stood and zipped up his pants. Then he put his hands in his pockets. 'My money, where's my money?' His money was gone. He had a whole $20.00 bill and it was gone. She stole my money. Tony warned me. He ran back up the flight of stairs, two at a time, and pounded on the door. The door opened and a gruesome, heavy set man with a stubby beard and tobacco stained teeth was standing there.

"Ya' want somethin'?"

When he looked beyond the door he saw Flo sprawled out on the bed, spread eagle and partially naked. When she looked up at him, she let out a wild laugh throwing her head back exposing herself even more.

"No. Nothing. Nothing."

Scared out of his mind, he scurried down the last flight of stairs and darted home at a fast clip. This was his first sexual encounter, and she stole his money. Lesson learned. When he got to his room he closed and locked his door, gasping and trying to catch his breath. He leaned up against the door, closed his eyes and let out a breath of relief. I could have been killed! I'm grateful to be alive. When he told Tony about it, he just laughed.

"Usually they get their money up front, maybe $2.00 but she scored big last night getting your whole $20.00."

"And I thought she liked me."

A few weeks later, Avak wanted to see more sights. He began to walk in unfamiliar territory. He knew he could find his way back home because the streets are numbered. But he was wrong. Down the bowery, the names of the streets were Mulberry Street, Canal Street and Barber Street, until he got so confused. Searching for a familiar site, he passed men shooting dice, in an alley, dollar bills in their hands. Gazing up at the sky and looking lost, he was jumped. Out of nowhere, came these thugs, just kids really; throwing him to the ground, punching him and searching for his wallet.

"Give me your money."

"Here, take it." He screamed back.

They hit him right in the eye, and he had difficulty focusing. What just happened? I'm lost and I lost all my money; another $20.00 gone. Here he was a grown man crying. Again he felt as if he didn't belong. Where can I go to be safe? Where can I go? Stumbling and focusing with one eye, he saw a sign that said 6th Avenue. Oh, I'm almost home. When he got to his apartment house, the superintendent, Alex, was at his desk, his office door open.

"What happened to you?"

"I got beaten up and robbed."

"Come into my office and I'll clean you up."

He went into the office and Alex, gave him some advice about where to go and where not to go alone. Unfortunately, it was a little late for that.

He left Alex's office and climbed the stairs to his room. Maybe I don't belong here either. Maybe there just isn't a safe place for me.

A year later, Tony came to Avak and told him about his cousin who was a shoemaker in Hartford, Connecticut. The store next to him was for rent and all set up for a tailor shop.

"Here's his number call him up if you're interested."

"Well, how about you?"

"No, I want to become a designer of woman's clothes. I have some sketches that I'm going to peddle and see if I can get a job here in New York."

"You thought of me?"

"Why wouldn't I? You're my friend."

He called the number on the paper and asked if it was still available. It was at $60.00 a month rent.

"Okay. I'll take it. I'll be there in a few days. I'll call you when I get in."

"Oh by the way, for another $20.00 a month you can have the apartment right next door."

"Great. I'll take that too. Thank you."

He asked Alex if he could use his phone and called his uncle to tell him. When Father Devletian came to the phone, he had some news for him, too. Father had been transferred to Canada where he was going to have his own parish.

"So, we are both leaving New York and starting all over again, huh?"

"You got me on the right road, Father. I have you to thank for everything."

"No son, you did it all on your own."

Father, my address will be 262 Sisson Avenue, Hartford, Connecticut"

"Let me write that down. I'll send you my mailing address when I get there. Good luck and, may God bless you."

"May God bless you, too."

Avak hung up the phone and he found himself crying. Alex asked him why was he crying?

"I don't know. I really love my uncle and I've never told him."

"You can tell him in a letter."

"Yes, you're right. That's what I'm going to do."

Avak gave his notice and packed his valise and left it on his bed. He went to Tony's rooming house to say good-bye. After walking up the flight of stairs he knocked on the door stamped #6 in green paint. The door opened and Tony was standing there as Avak looked beyond him and saw his opened valise on the bed packed with clothes.

"Are you going somewhere?"

"Please come in."

He walked in and Tony closed the door behind him.

"Avak, I'm in trouble."

"What do you mean?"

"Sit down. Something terrible has happened."

Avak sat on the corner of the very neatly made bed and didn't take his eyes off him.

"Tell me. What?"

Tony sat on the opposite side of the bed.

"Come on. Give."

"Well, I met a girl at the dance hall a few months ago. She went out with some buddies of mine as well as me. Yesterday she waited for me after work and said she had something to tell me."

"What was it?"

"She told me she was pregnant and said I was the father. But when I told my buddies about it they said she had gone to them and said the same thing. I can't imagine that it's me because I was careful. I can't stay here and take the chance that she blames me.

"So, what are you going to do?"

"I'm leaving town."

"What about your plans to become a designer?"

"I can't think about that. First things first, I'll worry about that later."

"Why don't you come with me to Connecticut?"

"No, no. I'm going back to Italy. When this all blows over, I'll come back. I'm going to try my luck in Milan."

"Is there nothing I can say to change your mind?"

"No, nothing, just wish me luck."

Avak felt really terrible. They embraced, slapped each other on the back and looked into each other's eyes. They had to control their tears. So much had transpired between them over the years. He had become a man under Tony's tutelage, and now Tony was in trouble and Avak couldn't even help him. He owed his new beginning to Tony, as well.

"I'll keep in touch through my cousin. I'll let him know where I am."

Avak opened the door and sadly left his friend. He went down the flight of stairs and walked to his rooming house as the wind began to pick up and the sky grew overcast. With his hands in his pockets he considered the change of events. Tony was his mentor, his link to New York and to his becoming a citizen. He was going to make his mark as a designer and now it was all blowing in the wind. But he's resilient. He'll be okay; I just have to believe that. When you play with fire you can get burned. It could have happened to me. A wrong move could change your life. Becoming a man is a life long journey.

Avak's very first order of business was to legally change his name. In his mind's eye he would change his name to George. George Avak. He would never forget he owed his life to a man name George. Yes, that was his first order of business.

He took his valise from the bed, checked the room over, and half smiled a good-bye, then went down the flight of stairs. He went to say good-bye to Alex. He was standing outside his office and Avak handed him his keys.

"Well, Alex, this is good-bye. Here's the rent for this week."

"Thank you. I'm going to miss you."

"I'm going to miss you too."

They shook hands, and Avak felt his eyes watery. He sniffed a little and tapped his forehead in a so long gesture, trying not to cry. Walking through the crowded street he hailed a hansom. The driver took his valise and helped him in the carriage. The horse was sleek with a red plume attached to his bridle. He felt special. This was his first and only hansom ride. Crossing over 5th Avenue, down Madison and then Park, this was part of New York that he had never frequented. The people on the street looked different. They were the ones wearing the suits and dresses that he probably made. Arriving at Grand Central, the driver handed him his valise and said, "That'll be two bits." Avak handed him the quarter and walked into the station.

He felt a sense of excitement and yet a pulling inside of him. He purchased a ticket and a newspaper, passing the shoeshine boy near the gate; with the slap, slap sound of his cloth. When he settled into his seat, he closed his eyes and thought, 'Why was I so emotional leaving Alex? I think it's what he represented. I spent many years in that apartment house in New York and now I was saying good-bye.'

So much had changed. His uncle had been transferred to Canada, his best friend was going to Milan, and he was on a new venture. He felt sad and happy at the same time. He loved New York, but now he would become the owner of his own business. It seems I'm forever saying good-bye; let's hope this is the last.

On the train ride, he started to have doubts. Could he do this? Did he know enough to run a business? He wouldn't know anyone. He was completely on his own. Fear settled in as the train chugged along, filling his head with apprehension.

CHAPTER 6

Virginia and Dorothy
Middletown, Connecticut

John called the girls into the living room. He was sitting on the over- stuffed, green velvet, chair. He asked the girls to have a seat across from him on the much abused slip- covered sofa.

"Ladies, I have made a decision."

"What is it now, John?" Virginia looked up, with boredom in her voice, rolling her eyes, legs crossed and swinging one in the beat of a hasapiko.

"You've been in the States for a few years now, and I have decided it's time for you girls to go to work."

"What? But we're still in school! You can't do this! Virginia screamed getting up from her chair.

"I fudged your records and made you a little older so that you would be eligible to work. They are hiring at the factory on East Main Street. You can walk both ways, and you don't even have to take a bus!"

"You can't do this. You didn't even ask us. We've made school friends. We love school. How could you do this to us?" Virginia, working herself up into a lather; anger brewing in the furrows of her brow.

"I'm having a difficult time meeting expenses; so you girls have to help."

"What do you mean you're having a hard time meeting expenses? You don't even work, and you're going to make us work. Why don't you work, John?"

"What's going on here?" Cynthia, rushed into the living room.

"Mom, John is making us go to work and not go to school."

Cynthia looked at John with disbelief. "John, did you really do this without my knowledge?"

"Mom, we need more money. You don't want to take in washing do you?" He said to her in Greek, to be sure she understood.

Dorothy, also angry, shouted, "What are you talking about?"

"You girls have learned enough. You'll like working. I'll let you have a few cents from your pay so you can go to the movies."

"If daddy were alive, this would never happen to us." cried Virginia, her face buried in her hands, still crying. You say you're the man of the house. A man would never make slaves out of his sisters. I hate you, giving him the 'go to hell sign' saying "na", five fingers spread apart with her palm toward him.

"Stop that Virginia. This is the first I've heard of this. John, how can we be in so much money trouble? You're the man. You have to get out there and get a job." Cynthia demanded; taking a table cloth from the drawer and slamming it.

"I have a job at the coffee house. They pay me when I work there."

"Yes, but, how often do you work there? I never see you go there." Her lips pursed, looking over the top of the rim of her glasses, hands on her hips.

"That's not the point. I have made up my mind. They are going to work. I am the head of this house and this is the only way. He got up and walked around the room like a dictator. He was breathing heavily now, sputtering profanities in Greek.

Cynthia went to the girls and stroked their hair. I'll talk to Andrew about this. Maybe he has a solution. "I don't really want to ask him because he has done so much for us already."

"You know Mom," John continued, "since Charlie and Tom left for California, we don't get any money from them."

Cynthia walked back to the kitchen, standing on the worn linoleum and stirring the pot of yogurt, contemplating her next move. She was not going to reveal her secret money she was saving for Theresa's voyage to America.

John strolled into the kitchen. "Don't worry, they'll get over it."

The girls started at the factory the following week, dreading the day they had to work. They were embarrassed to tell their friends that they had to work, but to their surprise there were others in the same predicament. They worked side by side, putting small items in boxes and performed other minor duties. The rooms were dark and dingy with very little light coming through tiny windows. They tried to catch glimpses of the weather outside through the dirty glass. They sat at long tables putting jars of glue in boxes getting 10 cents per box. Their mother made sandwiches for them, and off to work they went, passing their school friends along the way. Their former school chums taunted them when they saw them going to work. They, in their new shoes and dresses and, Ginger and Dorothy in their ill fitted second hand garb. Depression set in very quickly and they needed a way out.

"Dorothy, I hate this."

"I hate it too. Remember when we were in school, posters were advertising night school?"

"Yes, I remember."

"I've been thinking. What do you say we start going to night school? We could get really good at speaking, reading and writing in English and take some classes about American history. What do you say?"

"Let's do it."

"We'll go to the school and sign up after work."

The poster was still there inviting immigrants to night classes free of charge. When they went there the next day, they went into the school and asked, "Where can we sign up?"

"Here, sign your name and address here and be here Monday at 6:00 P.M."

"Okay." They walked out the door, ecstatic. John would never find out, they'd tell their mother where they would be so she could cover for them.

Walking home, they felt they had another chance at becoming Americans, and they had done it on their own. A big smile came over their mother's face when they told her.

"Maybe you'll meet some nice Greek friends there."

"Mom, we're not going there to meet Greeks. We're going there to learn what John wouldn't allow us to learn."

"I'm sorry. I just want you girls to have some friends."

"I know, Mom. We start on Monday right after work."

"I'm so proud of you for outwitting John. I wish I had thought of it for you."

When Monday night came they hurried to their class. They walked into the class room where Virginia had spent every day, her eyes fixed on her old desk. She looked around and felt a lump in her throat wanting those happy days. The class room started to fill with young and old; and from different countries. They were given notebooks with numbered lessons and exercises, all of which looked familiar.

To Virginia the beginning of the notebook looked easy, sort of a review. But as she flipped through, she realized how much she didn't know. Walking out of the school and looking at the brick building, there were reminders of their days there; like heart shaped graffiti with initials 'so and so loves so and so' and "Kilroy Was Here." written all over the outside of the building.

"I miss coming here. Virginia said sadly. "I remember the time Bobby pulled Roseann's hair and she screamed. Everyone knew he liked her but he had to sit in the back of the room, by himself, just the same."

After taking these classes, both girls felt they had one up on John - a secret weapon they could use if it became necessary. He thought he would be the only one who could write confidently in English and the girls were too stupid to accomplish what he had. Now they were his equal and could stand up to him if he forced another unacceptable change in their lives.

They were doing something together. Their mother was in on their secret. But, if John ever found out that they were still going to school there would be hell to pay for all three of them.

CHAPTER 7

Dorothy Mollis – Age 16

Since the time when the ancient Greeks worshiped the gods, marriages had been arranged. This tradition continued through the 20th century. It was expected one would marry someone Greek from their village. Love was never a consideration.

In the spring, Dorothy and her mother were suddenly invited to Mrs. Andonis' house for an afternoon coffee. Marriages were arranged through friends. That was called a proxinia, match making, coming from the word xenos which means friend. Cynthia was convinced there would be a suitor there, from Eressos, for Dorothy.

"I don't understand why Dorothy's invited and I'm not." whined Virginia.

"I don't know, it's only for coffee." Cynthia didn't want to reveal her suspicions to Virginia or to Dorothy.

The two girls and their mother went into the girl's bedroom looking for something appropriate for Dorothy to wear. When that was decided, Cynthia went to John and confided,

"I have a feeling Mrs. Andonis has someone for Dorothy to meet, I know she's only sixteen."

"I don't think anything is going to come of this. Dorothy doesn't show any interest in men yet." John supposed.

"We couldn't refuse the invitation could we?"

"No, no. It's really important, if it really is a proxinia."

In their bedroom, down the hall, Virginia and Dorothy fussed over re-evaluating the dress and shoes until they agreed on a light blue, sweetheart neck, full skirt number. Cream colored shoes would look fine with it. Dorothy pressed the dress and hung it on a hanger ready for tomorrow.

There weren't an abundance of choices in this department. They didn't have any money to spare. They had to make do with what they had. Virginia curled Dorothy's hair with the curling iron heated on the stove. She wore it back away from her face. She wasn't a beautiful girl but she had outstanding, porcelain skin and soft, gentle, brown eyes.

To Virginia, Dorothy looked perfect, and she was proud of her primping skills.

Cynthia wore a navy blue crepe dress, with the white collar; the only dress she owned that wasn't a house dress, given to her from Andrew and Angie. Her gold cross, which she never removed, glistened against the dark blue.

As Virginia stood in the doorway, she watched them leave, totally jealous for not being allowed to have this social interaction.

"Have a good time." Virginia waved, half-heartedly. Closing the door behind her, she thought, 'I really don't understand why I couldn't go. Mrs. Andonis is a mean woman, not to invite me. I hope they have a rotten time!'

Dorothy felt pretty walking alongside her mom for the two blocks up the street. This was a special time, just she and her mom together. They enjoyed this cloudless afternoon. The rustling of the young leaves in the trees made music through the gentle breezes. The cluster of daffodils had passed their prime and the tulip petals had already fallen. But the lilac bushes were in full bloom, and the fragrance was overwhelming. This put Dorothy in a wistful frame of mind and made her think of Theresa. She turned to her mother and asked,

"Have you heard anything from Aunt Chrisanthi about Theresa?"

"She sent a very disturbing letter yesterday saying that Theresa does not behave and we wouldn't want her here. I don't believe her, and I'm going to try everything I can to get her here. What's my baby going through there without us?" Thoughts of her Theresa, revealed Cynthia's worried expression, which she knew she must hide.

"What? I don't believe that. We have to do something to bring her here."

"I've been saving money, saving every penny, until I have enough to bring her home. I've never mentioned it to John. It's been my secret and I'm sharing it, with you. I'm afraid if John finds out, he'll take the money."

"I won't tell John, but can I tell Virginia?"

"Yes, you can tell Virginia."

Hearing the sound of Greek music coming through the open windows, mixed with loud chatter, they rang the doorbell, smoothing their clothes as they waited for the door to open. Anna Antonis came to the door and welcomed them warmly.

"Come in, come in. Hi, Dorothy, it's so nice to see you."

"Thank you for inviting me."

Anna's husband, Stavros, joined her and took Cynthia and Dorothy around to meet the other guests. The house was warm and charming, but, like theirs, a little worn.

Anna took them into the living room and they sat next to each other. The dining room chairs were mahogany, and placed around the living room to ensure ample seating. They knew most of the guests, but Dorothy still felt uncomfortable as the youngest in the room. She sat very ladylike in the chair and became increasingly self-conscious. She kept fidgeting with her imitation pearl bracelet and crossed and re-crossed her legs. She was purposely seated beneath a large painting of wild flowers.

More people kept coming, and friends and neighbors passed around the sweets and the coffee. Two men were walking around the dining room and the living room talking to guests, but periodically looking over at her. Every once in a while, the taller one smiled at her then leaned over and said something to Mrs. Antonis. Then he'd look over at her again. It became obvious that the taller one was invited to meet Dorothy. Anna continued to bring them to meet others at the party. Dorothy began talking to the woman sitting next to her, whom she met when she first came to America. She became increasingly suspicious as to why she was there; she felt like a fish out of water; a piece of meat on inspection at the local butcher shop.

Anna and her two male friends occasionally looked over at her, and continued to whisper. She really liked the looks of the shorter one but he wasn't looking at her.

When Dorothy looked up she saw the taller man and Anna coming toward her.

"Dorothy, I'd like you to meet Jack"

"Jack, this is Dorothy."

"Hello," Dorothy said shyly with her eyes examining the floor.

"It's nice to meet you," Jack said trying to look straight into her eyes but couldn't find them.

"Anna," he continued, "What a lovely painting."

"Yes, isn't it lovely?"

That was the code. If John liked Dorothy, he would compliment the painting above where she sat. Now it was time for Anna to proceed. She went over to Cynthia with Jack, introduced him, and it was decided that Jack would come to the house for a visit the following Sunday. Now Dorothy realized why she was invited. It was to meet this Jack. This was her proxinia.

She thought, 'I'm only sixteen and someone wanted to meet me. I can't wait to tell Virginia.'

When they got home, John was sitting in the parlor waiting for them. Cynthia told John of her plans for Sunday and all about Jack.

"He's coming here on Sunday?" John was unnerved!

"Yes, I invited him."

"I see." He pondered, rubbing his face with his hand then tapping his finger on his chin. "Hmm, what does he do for a living?"

"I don't know, but he's interested in Dorothy and he seemed very nice; one step at a time."

John went out on the front porch and lit a cigarette. He paced back and forth, deep in thought. It's good that Dorothy should marry. On the other hand, that would mean there would be less money coming in. He would have to figure something out. However, this Jack might have a really good job and could take care of all of them.

Oh no, wait a minute. He may ask for a dowry – then what would I do? We have nothing to offer him – not even a cow! I may have to go to work. Nah.

I guess I'll just have to keep depending on Andrew now that mother had a talk with him. He doesn't charge us rent for the apartment, and he lets us keep the money from the renters above us. We'll be all right. Having Dorothy gone will be one less mouth to feed. I'll be okay. I won't need a job. Phew, that was close! He finished his cigarette and walked back into the house and let out a sigh of relief.

Dorothy had already run to find Virginia.

"Virginia, Virginia, Where are you?"

When she found her, she was sitting alone, pouting.

"What are you doing? She jumped on the bed. "Don't you want to hear about this afternoon?"

"Yeah, okay, what?" she answered still sulking that she wasn't invited.

"There was a man there for me, his name is Jack."

"Oh my God, you're kidding." Now she was interested. "Tell me everything."

"What's he like? Did you talk to him?"

"No. Not, very much. This afternoon was all planned and I just sat there and everyone was gaping at me. I was wishing so much that you were there."

"Me too, but, tell me about him."

"He's coming next Sunday to meet everyone. I guess he's interested in me."

"You mean he's coming here? You mean he wants to marry you?"

"No, I didn't say that; it's just for a visit."

"Yeah, right, he wouldn't be coming if he didn't want to marry you. It's a proxinia for cripes sake. It's a visit for a proxinia, then! How do you feel about it?"

"I don't know. I've never had anyone pay attention to me before. I feel a little scared and lonely. It's like walking on ice but yet afraid it will break and I'll fall through and drown."

"Aw, I'll bet a dime to donuts John isn't going to like him."

"I really do want to get married someday, but I'm too young don't you think?"

"How old is he?"

"I don't know. But he's friendly with Mrs. Antonis and she's in her 30's."

"Do you think he's 30?"

"He sure looks it. He's already bald."

"Oh, no."

Dorothy crawled into bed that night, her head spinning. She had no idea how she was supposed to act in the company of a man. What if she says the wrong thing? What if Jack sees through John that he's lazy and out of work? What if he thinks our home is shabby? What if he asks for a dowry and we have nothing? With these frightening thoughts running through her head, she never slept.

Walking to work the next day, Dorothy told Virginia about the letter their mother received from Aunt Chrisanthi.

"Is she crazy? What is she doing to Tepsi? Dorothy, we have to do something to bring her home."

"We can take some money from our pay envelope and the spending money he gives us then give it to mommy. We can only hope that John doesn't notice. Mom's been saving every penny she can."

"Yes, but what if we get caught? What will we do? He'll accuse us of stealing. He could make life miserable for us." Virginia pressed.

"I know. I know. We've got time to think about it."

Jack came for visits every Sunday until he was ready to pop the question. This particular Sunday there seemed to be very little conversation until Jack asked Cynthia if he could take Dorothy for a walk around the block. She said yes, and when they came back Dorothy had a huge diamond ring on her finger. Everyone was excited and talking at the same time. John got up and poured some scotch, and the men had a drink. They talked about a wedding date and plans. Dorothy couldn't stop smiling. She kept looking at her hand and admiring the ring on her finger. Everyone was talking about the wedding, the wedding; who to invite. Dorothy enjoyed being the center of the attention showered upon her.

Virginia thought, 'I guess this is the way it's done here in America, too. Just like in Eressos. Nothing has changed, here. Coming to America didn't change anything for Dorothy, but it's not going to be like that for me. I'm choosing my own husband.'

That night, after Jack left, Virginia and Dorothy were readying for bed. Plunking herself on her bed, Virginia asked,

"Don't you want more out of life?"

"What do you mean?"

"Well, you meet this Jack, he comes over for a few Sundays, and boom you're going to get married? Do you think you love him?"

"I don't know. He seems nice enough. I'm paving the way for you to find a husband."

"Are you kidding? I'm only a kid. I've got years ahead of me to find the right person to send me to the moon. I'm not going to end up with a proxinia, not me."

"I want you to be excited and happy for me. Can't you just do that?"

"Okay, I'm sorry. If you want me to be happy for you, I will and I am. Now that I know this is what you want, I will never say another word."

'But, I know she'll be sorry.'

CHAPTER 8

Separation of Dorothy and Virginia

Jack was the exemplar of why the proxinia existed. For Dorothy and this immigrant family, he was the catch. He had a very good position in a large company and was moving up the ladder. Dorothy anticipated a typical Greek wedding. They would marry in the Greek Church in New Haven.

In their bedroom Virginia and Dorothy were getting ready for the big day.

"Dorothy, I wish Theresa could be here for your wedding."

"Luckily John didn't notice less money in our envelopes. You're going to have to continue to do it, now that I'm married and not going to work anymore."

"Of course I will. I'll even give a little more and hope he doesn't notice." Virginia smiled at her. "But I'll still be here all by myself."

"Oh stop it. You have Mom and John. You're not by yourself. You have to grow up, I have to."
"You're right. I have my whole life ahead of me to make my own choices."

The wedding was very Greek. Family and friends were all invited just as in Greece. Dorothy wore a white chiffon gown with tiny buttons all the way down the back, flouncy and feminine. She carried roses with white ribbon streamers. She looked like a princess, Virginia thought. She's starting a new life, now a wife, but Virginia couldn't help but feel Dorothy should have had more. She could be looking at John with adoration like they do in the movies, rather than looking down at her shoes, crying occasionally.

John walked up to her. "What's the matter with you, Virginia? You don't look happy for your sister. You're not jealous of her are you?" John provoked.

"Me? Jealous of what? Of being married off to the first person who shows interest? And, not being in love? I should be jealous of that?"

"Well, you could at least act as if you're having a good time."

"I'm not and I really want to go home."

After Dorothy left, Virginia continued night school. One night the instructor asked a question about why the first settlers came to America. Virginia raised her hand and said, "To find freedom of religion and freedom for individuals." Then a discussion ensued. She had started something. People were telling their stories about why and how they came here. It was one of the best nights. She was invigorated.

Then the instructor handed out loose-leaf notebooks. She said, "To familiarize yourself with the English language, I suggest that you keep a journal of your daily activities. It's just for you to keep and enjoy."

Virginia had never even entertained this concept. Writing down her own private thoughts that no one would know about. This was a gift from God. Why had she never thought of it? She could do something on her own, just for herself. She would be able to write all her secret thoughts that went against Greek tradition. She possessed a diary that was hers alone to keep and make a plan to break out. She would have to find a secret hiding place so no one would ever find it.

CHAPTER 9

Theresa's "Tepsi's" Homecoming

The loneliness Virginia felt persisted even though she wrote in her journal. However, it didn't replace the emptiness she felt, spending nights alone in her room. She dwelt on the times she spent with Dorothy when they were young, sneaking down to the neighbor's to swing on their swings; and when they would pick flowers from the empty lots to bring home to their mother. Going to work every day was torture. Going with Dorothy, gave her someone to share the misery with. She kept pestering John to do something to bring Theresa home.

"I'm trying, Ginger, I'm trying. It's not easy. We just don't have the money."

"John, you've got to do something. This has been going on too long."

"I'll handle it. You just mind your business."

"Sure, you're handling it and nothing has been done."

Virginia continued going to night school and working in the factory, continuing to sneak as much money as she could to her mother for Theresa.

Several months later, summer was just around the corner. Virginia was locked in her room, writing in her journal, oblivious of what was happening in the rest of the house. Cynthia had set the table using her mother's hand crochet tablecloth and Sunday dishes. A bouquet of forsythia was in a glass in the center of the table.

"Come on John, come on Virginia. It's time to eat."

Reluctantly, Virginia got up from her chair, hid her journal in its hiding place and sauntered down the hall for dinner.

"What's the special occasion, Mom? Why all the good stuff?"

"Just sit down. We're having lamb chops tonight with pilaf and yogurt."

"Lamb chops? There has to be a special reason."

"Come, come and eat."

John and Virginia sat and ate in silence, savoring every bite. It was a rare occasion to have lamb chops."

After they ate, Cynthia had an announcement to make. She placed a frayed cardboard box on the table. She said to Virginia,

"Open the box."

Virginia did as she was told and there were coin and bills piled high.

"Mom, you have enough money to send for Theresa?" She got up did a little dance.

"Yes I do. I have saved $30.00 for her. John, I want you to make the arrangements for Theresa to come home immediately! I have been saving money ever since we came to America, to bring Theresa home. I want to bring my baby daughter home."

"But, how did you get the money? I have been scraping and conniving and juggling to make ends meet. How did you do that?" John asked.

"Let's just say I did it. You don't have to know how. I had my priorities and you had yours. Just get it done."

"It's all making sense now. You never bought anything new; not even a new pair of shoes. You were always looking around for cardboard. Was that to put inside your shoes? You were always with a needle and thread, sewing your house dresses. That's what you were doing all these years?" John looked at her with such amazement and respect; and also with a little bit of fear at his mother's determination.

John stammered, "I'll arrange it immediately, Mother."

In six weeks time, Theresa arrived in New York. Mom, John and Virginia went to Ellis Island to meet her. They took the ferry to Ellis Island and went to the same room where Virginia waited for her dad. She remembered the emptiness and despair she felt on that day. How they waited and waited and then he never came. Still when she thought of it, she wondered, 'how could that have ever happened?' When they walked up the stairs, oh my God, there was Theresa waiting for them. She was very small yet so beautiful and so painfully thin. She had long, auburn hair and was as delicate as a wren.

"Tepsi, Tepsi," Virginia yelled.

She waved, then picked up her tiny suitcase and walked very slowly toward them. John took her valise and Tepsi collapsed in her mother's arms. Cynthia broke down and cried and cried, embracing her fourteen year old daughter. It had taken ten years to save the money to bring her home.

"I prayed every night for this moment. Oh my darling girl," she kept repeating.

On the train ride back to Connecticut, Theresa had something to eat that her mother brought. She slept, cradled in her mother's arms. They got in John's car and she slept all the way home until the car stopped in the driveway.

John carried her upstairs to Virginia's bedroom that Tepsi would share with her. Virginia took off her shoes and dress and covered her. She slept through the night.

The next morning, Theresa opened her suitcase. She gave Virginia a smile,

"I have something to give you. I've waited so long for this moment."

"What is it?" She said, leaning toward her.

Tepsi handed her a crumpled Greek newspaper and when she opened it, there was her clothespin doll, soiled and tattered, but still intact.

"Tepsi, you still have it?"

"Of course I do. Do you remember when we were on the ship and I couldn't come with you? You gave this to me to keep me from crying. It's the only doll I ever had. You said when I come to America I can give it back to you. Well, here she is. She's the only thing I had to hold on to during those lonely, horrible nights when I was little and, thinking of you and our family and what your life must be like here in America."

"Tepsi, I was worried about you and prayed you were okay."

"I'm okay. Don't worry about me; I'm okay now that I'm home."

"Last night was the first time I slept in a bed. I'm going to be sleeping in a bed!"

"What do you mean?"

"When I was little, I slept on blankets on the floor. When I got older I slept on a cot."

"You slept on the floor? Why? Do you want to tell me about it?"

"Yes, I will tell you, mom and John, all at the same time. It's too exhausting and painful to tell but once."

"I missed you so much. And you know what? I never expected you to be so beautiful. You are you know."

"You really mean it? No one has ever said that to me before", as her eyes widened. "You know what? On the ship was a big, big mirror, from the floor to the ceiling. I looked into it and saw myself for the first time. I never saw me before. I was surprised, I'm not so bad. Aunt Chrisanthe kept telling me that I was ugly."

"What? She said that to you? How could she say that?"

"Yes, all the time."

Mom called for breakfast. They held hands walking to the table.

"After you tell us everything, then you should take a nice hot bath.

"Oh that sounds wonderful."

"Come sit, Tepsi. Come and tell us everything. We are your real family," her mother said.

"Mommy, all the years that I was with Aunt Chrisanthe, she had me as a υπάλληλος, epallilos, a servant. I had to go to the well and pump the water, three times a day. I had to sweep the house in the morning and at night. Aunt Chrisanthi's son, Christos, hated me. He would tell his mother that I did the bad things he had done and then I was punished. She rarely let me go to school.

She had a sewing machine and she taught me how to sew. Then, she took in sewing. I would do all the work and the rich people would pay her but, she never gave me any money, ever. I cooked and I cleaned up every day. I did the washing. I had to use a scrub board."

"You had to use a scrub board? Let me see your hands, Virginia posed.

She spread her hands on the table and they were the hands of a σκλάβος, sklavos, a slave, not a fourteen year old's.

She continued, "And worst of all, when I would cry for you, Mommy, she told me that you didn't want me and that's why I couldn't leave Eressos."

John got up from the table and paced the floor. Rubbing his chin he screamed, "How could she do this? How could she? How could she do this to my sister?" He slammed his fist on the table and had a murderous look in his eyes. Cynthia and Virginia got up from the table and hugged and kissed her. Virginia stroked Theresa's hands as if that would make it all better.

"She gave Christos everything because he was her son, but nothing for me. They would leave me alone with instructions of what I had to do, and it better be done by the time they got home. Sometimes she would say that they didn't have enough food and I was eating their food. I never asked for anything, even if I was starved. After she did or said something to me, horrible, she would go into the next room and laugh. She even laughed when she told me that daddy had died."

"I knew you didn't know what I was going through. Every night I prayed that God would send for me. Sometimes I was so tired and hungry, I would pray that God would come and take me to be with daddy."

Her mom, still crying, smoothed her hair and hugged and kissed her, whispering, "chrisaumou, my sweet" repeatedly. "Your life begins now. Forget everything that has happened as best you can. I will do everything I can to make it up to you."

Virginia went to work and Theresa had a nice hot bath and washed her hair. Andrew and Angie came down stairs to greet Theresa and brought her some dresses and shoes. She squeezed the dresses close to her and she tried on the shoes, this was the best day! Oh how different to be among family that loved her!

"Look, Mommy, the shoes fit me. Thank you, thank you," still not letting go of the dresses.

Virginia left for work, as usual. It was a warm, sunny day and she was happy that Theresa was her roommate. She said good morning to her bench mates and went about her work. Taking a bathroom break, she had to go down the hallway and down the dark cement stairs at the end of the hall. When she came out there was a man standing there, blocking her way to the stairs. She went to walk past him but, he grabbed her arm and said,

"Hey, girlie, ya'wanna have some fun?"

She tried to break away, but he was too strong. Kicking and biting, she fought back. As she struggled to get away, he tore at her blouse and ripped it in half. She kept digging her nails into him and she let out a blood curdling scream.

He let go of her and she ran down the hall and up the stairs, shaking and crying, hysterically, trying to hold her blouse together. When she got to her station, the women hovered around her. Her supervisor came to her and said, "Oh my God, you poor kid. Come and sit down in my chair."

"No" she protested. "I just want to go home."

"Do you know the man who did this?"

"No. But I've seen him before."

"Did he have a big scar across the top of his forehead?"

Virginia nodded her head yes.

"I'm going to report this, immediately. Let me have one of the girls walk you home."

"No. I just want to run home."

She left her pocketbook and lunch and ran home without turning back. Virginia ran up the stairs, into the house, crying and torn. When she told them what happened, John went ballistic. His face darkened into something Ginger had never seen before.

"What?" We'll go to that factory in the morning, get your pay and you'll quit! No one touches my sister! How dare he? I want to find out who he is. I'll rip him apart, that no good bastard!"

John could take advantage of his sisters but, no one else could. Virginia thought, 'He really does care about me. But, now I'm never going to see my friends at work anymore because of something that wasn't my fault?'

The next day, John accompanied Virginia to the factory. He went into the office and registered a complaint. They all knew what had happened.

"I want her pay envelope and she is quitting. I want this man's name."

"Now, now, sir, we know who did this and we have fired the individual and have notified the police. You don't have to go any further. We are very sorry for what happened to Virginia. She doesn't have to quit."

"Yes she does. Come on Virginia. We're going home."

Virginia had nothing to say. She was perplexed. He wanted her to quit and yet we needed the money. What happened to me was all his fault, in the first place.

On the way home, John put his arm around her.

"I'm so sorry you had this happen to you, sis. I think it's time for us to move. What do you say we move to Hartford? It's bigger than Middletown. I think we're ready for a move. What do you think?"

"Okay." But, she wondered, 'What did he really have up his sleeve.'

The new home located on Franklin Avenue in Hartford was a furnished two family house. Everything was on one floor, but it sort of looked the same as the Middletown rental. It was a first floor apartment with the bedrooms in the back, a big kitchen, a big dining room and a front room with a very large bay window. There was a front porch in need of paint with two rocking chairs, past their prime. It looked rather inviting in a rundown sort of way.

John seemed to be very excited about this move and Virginia couldn't figure out why. However, it didn't take her long to find out that John had a girlfriend in Hartford who had a job. Her name was Eleanor, but we never mentioned her. We acted as if we didn't know he had a girlfriend. After all, she wasn't Greek!

CHAPTER 10

Hartford, Connecticut

Living on Franklin Avenue made it easy to take the trolley into downtown to work. Virginia had been working at the S&A Department store for over a year now, and had made some good friends. The store was very big and carried every household item imaginable. It had very large windows, from the floor to the ceiling displaying the merchandise to those who walked by. There were cash registers located at each of the six counters. The ceilings were very high, painted white, with hard wood floors. It was an immaculate, inviting store.

The girls at work were about her age, in their early twenties, and very American. Virginia wanted to be just like them. Greek upbringing and not having a father had many drawbacks. How she wished she could be like the other girls, wearing makeup, bangle bracelets and going out on dates.

But she did her work and took the trolley back home each night, dreaming of becoming just like those girls.

In the ladies room, after lunch, she overheard the girls making plans to go to the pavilion on Friday night. When she got home she confided in Theresa.

"Gee, Thepsi, I wish I could be like the girls I work with. They go out on dates and dance and have such a good time."

"Don't worry about it, Virginia. John will find a husband for you any day now."

"But I don't want a proxinia. I want to find my own husband. Plus I want some excitement in my life."

"You know that isn't possible. You have to follow tradition. Just like me."

"No I don't. I am not going to do what Dorothy did. I'm going to find my own husband and in the meantime, I'm going to have some fun."

"Oh God, Virginia, what are you going to do?"

"I don't know exactly, but it's going to be something."

That night when Virginia wrote in her journal, she spelled out her desire to become an American. She wanted the freedom of the girls she worked with. She wanted to wear lipstick and high heels and nice dresses. She wanted to be just like them.

She wrote in her journal. This is my dream. I want to dress up like an American girl. I want people to turn their heads when I walk by. I don't want them to see a foreigner from Greece. I want them to say, "Hey, look at that American girl dressed in high heel shoes and a fancy dress." Then, I'm going to find the man of my dreams, all by myself.

Friday came and Virginia was listening to the girls making their plans to meet at the pavilion in Colts Park, as they were putting on their make up in the ladies room.

"Corrine, I'll meet you and May at the pavilion tonight at 8:00 okay?"

"Sure, Connie, we'll be there. I hope we have as good a time as we did last Friday night. That was just swell!"

"I'm sure we will. Hey, Ginger, do you want to meet us too?"

"You mean me?"

"Yes, we'd love to have you come."

"What do you actually do there?", she asked, all flustered.

"We listen to the music from the big band and sometimes we dance."

"Do you think you could show me how to dance?"

"Of course we will!"

"Okay. See you at 8:00," hiding her enthusiasm.

All the way home on the trolley she wondered how she was going to pull this off. What would she say to the family and where would she say she was going?

The girls were drying the dishes as Virginia told Theresa of her plan. They would go to their room, saying they were tired, and Virginia would climb out their bedroom window and go to the park.

"But Virginia, what if you get caught?"

"So what's John going to do, kill me or take my pay which he already does? You have to cover for me. I'll put my pillow sideways under the covers, just in case someone comes into the room. John will be out and mom usually falls asleep crocheting or sewing and listening to the radio."

"Virginia, I'm nervous."

"Why? Look, if anyone comes in and wakes you, just say you have no idea where I am, okay? I'll face the music if that happens. Don't worry."

"Okay, but hurry back. Try to get home before John does."

"Okay, leave the window open."

Virginia opened the window, threw her shoes out first then shimmied down catching her skirt on the drain pipe. Whispering in a gagging throat, "Theresa help me, I'm stuck." Theresa came running. Held her hand so she could free her skirt then she jumped down on to the ground. "Thanks. Don't forget to keep the window open a little for me." She checked for damage to her dress, slipped on her shoes and ran from her home to Wethersfield Avenue. The star lit sky gave way to a promising evening. Following the melodious sounds of the band, she hurried until she was out of breath. She weaved in and out of bushes and parked cars. She was anxious to get there and worried that John might be driving on the Avenue and see her. When she got there, she just stared at the men and women and how nicely they were dressed. She thought to herself, the girls are right the band is huge; horns, drums, accordion, violins – and a girl singer, as well. You name it, they've got it!

She searched around the pavilion and finally spotted the girls, waving to her to join them.

"Isn't this fantastic? Look at you. You're all out of breath."

"I know, I ran all the way. Whew, let me catch my breath." She didn't want the girls to realize that she was sneaking out; that her life wasn't as free as theirs. But she did want them to know she was happy to be included.

"Come on let's get on the dance floor and dance the night away."

"Oh, no, I'll just watch." Virginia protested pulling back.

"It's easy." Corrine shouted. "Just watch me."

They held hands and rushed to the dance floor. Swaying to the music, Virginia tried to keep up but they were too quick for her. She stumbled around the floor and fell. She hit the wooden floor with a crack! Her knees stung and when she got up she was bleeding. She wiped the blood with a hanky from her purse. It wasn't too bad, and she ran to catch up with the girls. They danced and danced and laughed and laughed; even the street lights looked special tonight. She felt a sense of freedom she had never experienced before, like emerging from a cocoon. Dancing without having anyone looking or judging her gave her hope that she could figure out how to implement her freedom. 'I can be free. I can be my own person. I just have to fight for it.' However, just as for Cinderella, the clock was approaching the witching hour.

"What time is it?"

"10:00"

"Okay girls, I have to get home. Thanks for teaching me to dance. I had a great time."

"Oh yeah, we have to go, too. Hope you can make it the next time we come."

"Thanks."

They all hugged good bye and Virginia turned and left. She felt that this was the first step in becoming like them. They had allowed her to join them, and she wanted so much to be a part of it. May seemed the nicest and helped her with the dance steps. She ran as fast as she could all the way home up and down hills. Up to this point, she had ignored the pain she was feeling in her knee. It was late. She got to Franklin Avenue, keeping her head down, hoping not to see anyone she knew. She was getting out of breath and began to walk more slowly, holding on to her knee, creeping lowly behind the bushes to the back of her house. She climbed up the side of the house just as her shoe fell off with a thud. 'Now what am I going to do?' She jumped back down, searching for her shoe on her hands and knees. She finally found it and tied both shoes by the laces and held them in her hand. She scrambled back up and pushed the window open wider with her free hand. Theresa had left the window open, just as she asked. She had to catch her breath before she hiked herself up and rolled in, onto the floor. She quietly put down her shoes and examined the damaged knee. It hurt but it had stopped bleeding. She removed her clothes, found her nightgown under the pillow where she left it. She put it on, quietly, threw her clothes underneath the bed and gently climbed in. She looked over at Theresa – sound asleep. 'Ahh – I did it! I made it! I'm home!' She secretly pulled her journal from the mattress and wrote, "No one belongs to me – but me. I'm leaving old shores and discovering new land."

In the morning, Theresa shook her awake.

"Get up. Get up. It's Saturday and you have to get to work."

She opened her eyes, music still singing in her head. The morning sun gleamed through the tops of the trees reflecting the serenity Virginia felt.

"Okay, okay, I'm coming."

She got dressed quickly, she had breakfast, exchanged a sheepish smile with Theresa. Before she could run to catch the trolley, her mother put her hand on Virginia's arm.

"Is there anything you want to tell me, Virginia?"

"No. Nothing."

"Are you sure? Well, if you think of something, you'll be sure to let me know."

"Yes. Sure."

Now she wasn't sure if she got away with it or not. What if her mother knows? What if she tells John? What if Tepsi told her? What if she checked my bed and I wasn't there?

Oh God.

111

CHAPTER 11

The Inevitable Comes to Pass

That night when she got home from work, John was sitting in the living room with a strange man.

"Virginia, come in here, please." He called firmly.

She walked into the parlor tentatively. "I'd like you to meet someone." as the two men rose to greet her. "This is Theodore. Theodore, this is my sister, Virginia."

"Hello." She said shaking his hand.

Virginia sat in the faded, flowered chair and smiled her best sincere, insincere smile, clenching her teeth.

"Theodore is from Eressos and he's just arrived in this country."

"Swell."

"He speaks English but is more comfortable with Greek."

"Swell."

John continued his conversation in Greek telling him that his sister is the girl he wanted him to meet. She's single.

"He's coming with his family tomorrow for coffee. It will be nice to meet some compatriots from home, don't you think?"

"Swell," She continued, with her artificial smile. "It's nice to meet you, Theodore. See you tomorrow." She got up and walked into the kitchen. John shot her a disgusted look and left with Theodore abruptly.

She slammed her pocketbook on the kitchen table.

"Is he kidding? He doesn't even speak English! Ahg, he's very Greek looking. He has a big nose, smoke stained teeth and not very tall. I will not be home tomorrow."

"Where do you think you'll be going tomorrow?" Her mother asked.

"I don't know, but not here." She stormed to her room. Theresa followed.

"Virginia, you should at least try to get to know this guy."

"Oh my God, I'd rather die. Where did John find him? It's not going to work. No, no, no!" her eyes beginning to well up and biting her bottom lip.

Cynthia was setting the table for dinner. She was hoping that Theodore would stay for dinner but Virginia was so rude, John didn't ask him to stay. She had made stuffed grape leaves and baked chicken with lemon potatoes. It was such a nice dinner it would have been nice to share it.

When John came back, Virginia was missing from the dinner table.

"Virginia, come here."

Defiantly, she walked into the kitchen. The table was set for the four of them. Tepsi was already sitting in her chair.

"Look, Virginia, you're twenty-two years old." John said, as he began to pass the chicken and potatoes around the table. "You're holding Theresa back from getting married. This is the third person you have rejected. Time is getting short for both you and Tepsi. I can't find a husband for her until you are married. Do you understand that?"

"I've told you I want to find my own husband." The food smelled so appetizing, she no longer

114

wanted to skip supper. She filled her plate with the food and began to dig in.

"Where are you going to do that?"

"How can I do anything? You don't let me go out."

"Where out? Don't be ridiculous!"

"Bring someone for Theresa, I won't mind."

"Do you want to become an old maid?"

"I like my life just the way it is. I don't need someone just to make you happy."

"Do you think you can live on your salary? You need a man to take care of you."

"Then I'll become a nun."

"Oh God," John rolled his eyes, and everyone laughed.

"Look, John, we live in America. I'm an American. I'm not going backward. This Theodore hardly speaks English."

"You should be thinking of your family. You should be married by now. What are people going to say?"

"Oh, I should live a life of misery to please my family? Are you nuts?"

"From where are you learning these words?" –
Swell - Are you nuts? Where is this coming from?"

She didn't answer. All of a sudden her appetite
vanished.

"Well, Theodore and his family are coming
tomorrow, and that's that."

Virginia took a deep breath, walked to her
room and slammed the door.

The next afternoon Theodore and his family
came. Virginia decided she had no choice but to be
there. She didn't want to insult her mother. She
would be just as rude as she was the previous day.

At the afternoon coffee both families discussed
Eressos and the families they each knew there,
blah, blah, blah. Then Theodore mentioned a Greek
dance coming up at the Hotel Bond. Virginia's ears
perked up. Theodore's family was planning to go,
and John sounded interested. She loved Greek
dances, and now she knew how to ballroom dance,
too. 'I need a new dress.' After they left, Virginia
cornered John, "Are you actually planning to take
us to the dance?"

"Of course I am. I'll do anything to get you a
husband."

"Then, I'll need a new dress and you have to
help me get one."

"Well, find one and let me know how much it
is; then we'll see."

Each day when Virginia got off the trolley on her way to work, she passed a clothing store that had a crepe, crimson red gown in the window. Every day she would look at it and wish she had a place to go to wear that gown. Well, now she had a place to go and how much she wanted that gown.

"Mr. Terwilliger, would it be okay if I went next door on my lunch time? I want to try on the dress in the window."

"Sure. Go ahead."

"May, come with me."

"Okay."

She went next door with May.

"I would like to try on that red dress in the window." The excitement in her voice was obvious. "How much is it?"

"Four dollars and certainly, you can try it on." The young man said. He was rather tall but mousy and had glasses down on his nose.

"Don't you work next door?"

"Yes I do."

"I see you every day coming to work," letting her know he noticed her.

"Oh." She said, not knowing what else to say.

117

"Here, take the dress into the changing room. My name is Bob Gray. Just ask for me when you've changed into the dress."

She was so nervous. Her hands were sweaty and clammy. She quickly changed and walked out to the open area where there was a three way mirror. She put her hands on her hips and eyed herself.

"Oh Virginia, it's so beautiful. I love the sweetheart neckline, it's so flattering. And the bows on the puffy sleeves add a special touch. It hugs your body in all the right places. It's you Virginia. It's really you." May gushed.

"Yes, but it's too long."

Bob Gray walked over and took a look at it and said his seamstress could shorten it but it wouldn't be ready for a week.

"That means it would be the Friday before the dance, and the dance is on Sunday." Virginia pondered rubbing her chin with her hand.

"We'll try our best to be ready on Friday."

"What will I do if it's not ready by Friday?"

"Just hope and pray it will be ready." May reassured.

Again on Sunday Theodore came to call. Virginia was very polite and used her almost forgotten Greek to appease John. She would have to make her move, but would wait until after the dance. The family is so looking forward to it, she wouldn't spoil it. They thought she was happy about the dance because of Theodore, but that was far from the truth. She had a new dress, and she was going to the best hotel in Hartford, The Hotel Bond. That was more than enough for her.

When she went back to the store to pick up the dress, it wasn't there.

"But Mr. Gray said it would be ready today. Friday he said."

"You'll have to wait until tomorrow when Mr. Gray comes back to work. He's off today."

"Okay. I'll come back tomorrow." She sighed, dejected. 'What if it isn't ready? What am I supposed to do?"

"I don't know the clerk said. You'll just have to wait until tomorrow."

This dress was so important to her. She just couldn't believe it wasn't ready.

"What if they don't have it tomorrow? I'll just die." And she fought to hold back her tears.

But, the next day, Virginia went back to the store, on her lunch break, after a night of not being able to sleep.

"Is Mr. Gray in?"

"Yes, he's in the back, I'll get him for you." The clerk answered.

He came to the front of the store.

Mr. Gray, is my dress ready?"

"Oh yes. Let me get it for you."

"Thank you." She let out a sigh and clasped her hands to her chest, whispering, thank God.

He came back with her dress and Virginia almost cried.

"Thank you. Thank you." She handed him the $4.00 John had let her keep from her pay.

"I'm sorry it wasn't ready for you yesterday. I hope you have a great time in your new red dress." He said, taking her $4.00 and smiling sheepishly at her. Virginia ignored it, took the dress and thanked him again and left the store.

CHAPTER 12

The Momentous Dance
And Her Red Dress

Theresa and Virginia were sitting demurely in the back seat of John's two-seater. It was a breezy winter night but spring was definitely in the air; clear and crisp. The stars twinkled against the sapphire sky.

"I'm sure Dorothy and Jack are already there, saving a table for us." Cynthia said, she seemed confident that this evening would be promising for Virginia and Theodore.

Theresa nudged Virginia,

"Holy Toledo, Ginger, you look fabulous." as if seeing her for the first time.

"Tepsi, you look pretty smashing, too. We're going to have a great time tonight."

"I sure hope so."

Actually Theresa did look especially beautiful tonight. Her taffeta, rust color dress matched the color of her auburn hair caught up in a sparkly barrette, allowing her curls to flow freely over her shoulders, but the tight curls around her face refused restraint.

Ginger gave Tepsi a squeeze, "We're going to the Bond." She shrilled almost not believing it. Who knows, you may meet someone here tonight."

"You think I might meet someone? I doubt it."

"I always wondered what the Hotel Bond's ballroom was like and now I am going to see it in person. The girls at work say it's spectacular. Look, Tepsi, look how tall the building is and, look at the majestic arched windows. There are ivy plants everywhere. My friend at work says it costs $3.00 a night to stay here in a room with a private bath."

John parked the car on the street and they walked across to the hotel. Virginia began to feel her stomach flutter just being in this beautiful place. Tonight even the stars were dancing. They walked into the spacious lobby where palm trees sat at the base of each column. The excitement for Virginia began to build as she watched the men and women so elegantly dressed in their long gowns and tuxedos. They took the elevator to the vestibule on the second floor. John handed the check girl their coats. He took the ticket, and they went down the open staircase where the ballroom was in full view. Ginger felt extraordinary walking down the stairs to the grand ballroom. The ceiling was about forty feet high; the floor was parquet. Large round tables with white linen table cloths were set-up all along the perimeter of the room, allowing a spacious dance floor. To be at such a gorgeous place was like a dream to Virginia.

"Theresa, look at the center pieces. Aren't they gorgeous?"

"Yes, look, the napkins match the table cloth."

"I'll bet they're expecting at least 300 people tonight."

Dorothy and Jack were already there saving a table, waving to them. They greeted each other and the men went to the bar to get some soft drinks for the ladies.

"My, you ladies look fabulous tonight," smiled Dorothy.

"Thank you. You look wonderful tonight too. Is that a new dress?"

"Yes, do you like it?"

"Yes, I do like it. Don't you think mine is swanky?" Virginia asked, spinning around.

"We'll certainly be able to find you, Ginger."

"I'm ready for a good time tonight," ignoring the backhanded compliment.

She looked across the room and saw a customer of hers, Mrs. Adajian, with a man who must be her husband. She shops at the S&A and owns the Round Table Restaurant on Asylum Avenue. Ginger thought she was captivating. She wore her hair like her mother, only hers is curly and the curls find their way through the braids around her head and give her a soft look rather than severe. Her eyes are sparkling black, rosy cheeks, the whitest teeth, and she always wears pearls; maybe because her name is Pearl. Every time she comes into the store, Virginia stares at her. She's warm, friendly and sweet.

"Mother, I'm going to go over and say hello to a customer who comes into the store, okay?

"Okay."

"Come on, Tepsi, come with me."

They walked across the ballroom to say hello to Mrs. Adajian. She recognized Virginia right away and introduced her to her husband. Virginia introduced Theresa, and Mrs. Adajian invited them to sit for a minute. Her children were young and seemed excited to be at their first dance. They too had black curly hair and big dark eyes and were dressed very special for the occasion. Pearl got up and hugged Virginia and told her how nice she looked and hoped she would have a good time tonight.

"Thank you. I always look forward to seeing you when you come into the store. I hope you have a nice time tonight, too."

They smiled and said good-bye. Walking back to the table Virginia said, "Isn't she beautiful? I just love it when she comes into the store."

"Yes, I can tell you really like her."

"I do. I really do. There's just something about her that draws me to her. I want to look just like her when I'm her age."

The band began to play and within minutes the dance floor was crowded. Because Greek dancing is line dancing, you don't need a partner to dance. The main instrument is the clarinet. Virginia couldn't wait to get on the dance floor. She felt so spectacular in her red dress.

"Come on, Tepsi, let's dance."

They both went to the dance floor and began to dance. They were playing an hysapiko which is 1,2,3 kick step kick, arm over arm dance to an up - beat tempo.

After they danced and giggled and the music stopped, they sat down to have a sarsaparilla and eat some appetizers that the waitress had served.

"I really love this band, don't you, Dorothy?" asked Virginia, breathing heavily.

"Yes, but don't get too warm now, Virginia." Dorothy warned.

Ginger whispered to Theresa, "She's always worried that I won't look my best; especially now that Theodore is coming to the dance."

Theresa and Virginia were just catching their breath when a young man came over to the table. He introduced himself to Theresa.

"Do you remember me?" He asked.

"I don't know. You look familiar but I can't place you."

"I'm Chrisanthi's brother, Costas. I remember you from Eressos."

"Oh yes, I remember you now." She said, her eyes widened like walnuts and her hands began to shake.

He pulled up a chair, sat next to her and continued.

"I recognized you and I wanted to come over and extend my apologies to you for the way my sister treated you. I am so sorry for all you endured. I just want you to know how much I hurt for you all those years. Chrisanthi is a very unhappy woman. Her son, Christos, has left Eressos and her husband has left her, too. She is totally alone, now."

"And, you never wanted to help me?"

"I couldn't. I'm your age. What could a kid do? Even though I complained to my mother, she said it was none of our business."

"I see", Theresa said quietly as her eyes narrowed. "I never want to see you again. You only remind me of your sister and there is nothing that can be said or done to make up for how I suffered. Now please leave." Now, she was trembling.

John looked over from across the table and came over to them, concerned.

"What's going on here?" John demanded.

"My name is Costas, and I'm Chrisanthe's brother. I just came over to say hello to Theresa and apologize for my sister's behavior."

"She doesn't need your apology. You think you can say you're sorry and that's going to make what she did okay? Get the hell outa here! We're here to have a good time and not deal with unspeakable memories." He seemed frightened when he left the table as John didn't take his eyes off of him until he was out of sight.

As Virginia was sipping her drink, the music started up again. She looked up at the vestibule and there coming down the stairs, was this gorgeous man in a tuxedo. He was very tall and stood very erect. He had black wavy hair combed back without a part. When he rounded the corner of the stairs to enter the ballroom, he had the most handsome face she had ever seen, as if he just

127

stepped out of a dream or a movie. Just the way he carried himself stirred something inside of her. She thought, 'Who is he?' He walked directly across the ballroom in her direction. She felt her heart skip a beat and her face flush, but as he came closer he took a right turn and headed directly to Mrs. Adajian's table. 'Oh', she thought. 'This must be someone they know and he's joining them. She wondered if he worked at the Round Table.'

Now she couldn't concentrate on anything. She found herself trying to steal glimpses of him without anyone noticing. Her mother motioned to someone at another table to join them. When she looked up, she saw Theodore and his mother and father coming over to their table with John. He wasn't wearing a tuxedo but a black suit that didn't quite fit. He said hello and Virginia said hello back, and then he asked her to dance. The band was playing a Tzimbekiko which is a two by two creative dance that requires interpretation for the music. Two men can dance, two ladies can dance, or a lady and a man can dance to it.

Everyone is waiting for her answer, so she says, "Sure." They started dancing and Theodore was not a good dancer at all. 'Well, that's another mark against him.' They were dancing opposite each other, arms up and snapping their fingers. While she's dancing, out of the corner of her eye, she noticed that young, handsome man was watching her. So, she put even more emphasis in her steps. Then she saw Mr. Adajian dancing with this handsome man. Everyone stopped dancing and all eyes were on them. He had spectacular moves. He barely moved his feet, as he moved to the music. Someone handed him a glass half filled with water. He balanced it on his head as he danced; bending and turning, while still balancing the glass. Then he shifted his balance from one foot to the other and lifted his foot, in front of him and brushed it with the back of his hand. How can he do that? Who is he? There were gasps and applause from the onlookers. An intense sensation passed through her body. She felt herself beginning to perspire and her face was turning red; she was feeling faint. Theodore noticed and asked,

"Virginia, are you feeling okay?"

"Oh, yes, I'm fine, do you mind if we sit down?"

"Of course not, I'll just sit right here next to you."

She thought to herself, 'This is a mistake. Now what am I going to do with him for the rest of the night? He can't even dance.' The buzz going through all the tables was about this newcomer who had just put on a highly charged, dramatic dance exhibition.

Her mother gave her a strange and knowing look. John was glaring at her over his eyebrows, arms folded across his chest just waiting for her to make a wrong move. He's just sitting at the table like a chief.

Her mother turned to her and said sternly, "Virginia, come with me to the powder room, please."

She didn't ask. It's an order, her tone revealed it. Mother took her arm and they walk straight to the powder room smiling and waving to people they knew. The powder room was not quite empty so they waited. The lighting in the powder room goes across the top of the full wall mirror. She checked herself in the mirror with approval. After a few minutes her mother started,

"Virginia, it is your duty and obligation to be respectful and pleasant to Theodore."

"But I am, Mother." without much conviction.

"No you are not," she protested angrily.

"But Mother, he can't even dance. I don't like him."

"You don't know him yet, how can you say that? Keep your place. I'm going to invite them for coffee next Sunday, and you'll get to know him much better."

"I don't want to get to know him better."

"Yes, you do and you will – and that's that. Keep your eyes to yourself."

Her mother stormed out of the ladies room as Virginia was trying to calm down and fix her hair, looking into the mirror. She noticed one of the stall doors opening very slowly. Out came her friend, Marianna.

"I overheard your conversation with your mother and I waited until she left before I came out. I have something that I want to tell you."

"What is it?" She asked, perplexed.

"Don't do it. I'm telling you, don't go for the proxinia." She pleaded. "I did and I'm miserable. I hate him. I don't know how to get out of it. I want to run away."

"Oh My God. You can't do that! Why are you so unhappy?"

"I came home from work and found him in bed with a waitress that he works with."

"Oh My God! Does your mother know?"

"Yes, she knows but she said I have to put up with it. "He'll get over it." She said. I'm telling you I can't live like this. I just want to run away. He married me so he could take over my father's diner."

"Oh, Marianna, I'm so sorry for your troubles. I had no idea. I don't know what to say."

"I'm just telling you. Find your own husband. Don't listen to your family."

Walking back to the table Virginia thought, 'my fate is before me. Do I do as I'm told, or do I try to find a way out? I'm sure mother noticed the way I reacted to the newcomer and that's why she brought me to the powder room for a good talking to.'

She looked over at John. He had an impatient look on his face. Like, 'get going and pay attention to Theodore.' She was sure they both noticed her reaction to this striking man. But she couldn't help it. Dorothy was giving her the evil eye, too.

Theodore asked, "Virginia, are you feeling better? Would you like to dance?"

They were now playing a waltz and her mother gave her a stern look.

"Oh yes, I'm much better, I'd love to dance." She says, giving him her perfect smile through clenched teeth. Now he's stepping all over her feet and trying to maneuver like Fred Astaire, but he's more like Donald Duck. His mother and father are watching them and smiling with approval.

"I think my mother likes you."

She smiles and says, "That's nice."

She gave her mother a look, looking for her approval of her demeanor.

Murdering the waltz as they were, on the dance floor is this gorgeous man again dancing with a young beautiful woman. Not only can he dance Greek, but his waltz is as smooth as silk, not fancy but just very, very smooth. 'How I wish I were dancing with him.' She looked up and saw Dorothy, with her arms folded under her breasts, staring at her, watching her every move just like John. She's the enforcer of her mother's demands. 'Oh brother, I'd better behave or the ride home is going to be torture.'

She was certain he noticed her and she certainly noticed him. I think he's the one I've been waiting for all my life. He's the man of my dreams. I'll dream of him tonight and just maybe it will come true.

CHAPTER 13

Day Dreaming

Busying herself at work, on this sunny morning, two weeks after the dance, Virginia still couldn't get this man out of her mind, constantly day dreaming; giving her a warm fuzzy feeling. Her mother had had the afternoon coffee for Theodore and his family as planned. Several Eressosian families came, too, and brought Greek pastries and the table looked quite appetizing. The guests were making obvious glances at Theodore and her during the afternoon. As usual, she and Theresa were the drones: serving, clearing, washing the dishes, in and out of the kitchen. The only conversation was in Greek about politics and the financial struggles in Greece.

Theodore's family was nice, causing her more guilt. They seemed to be appraising her during this obligatory afternoon. John and Theodore were head to head on the sofa enjoying each other's company. John liked him because he was from Eressos.

After the guests left, questioning eyes were on her. She just rolled her eyes, exhaled and routinely picked up some more dishes and walked into the kitchen. Theresa followed.

"Virginia, do you want to tell me what's on your mind?"

"Tepsi, this is a charade. I can't go through with this"

"We all agreed that this is a perfect match for you. Take it one step at a time."

"No, I can't do it. I didn't agree." Her lips were quivering now.

"Why? Give me a reason."

She put her head down knotting her fingers together, "Because, I'm in love with someone else."

"How can you be in love with someone else? You don't even go out on dates. Where did you meet this person?"

"Well, I've never actually met him," averting her eyes.

"You're saying that you're in love with someone and you've never even met him?" Are you talking about someone in the movies or someone in your dreams?"

"I just saw him and I know he's the one for me. I just know it."

"Is he from Eressos?"

"I have no idea where he's from and I don't really care."

"Where did you see this person?"

"At the dance at the Hotel Bond," she mouthed.

"Who could that be?"

"I saw him and I think he saw me, too. He was very tall and handsome and could really dance."

"Oh, you mean the one who was dancing and everyone stopped to watch."

"Yes, he's the one, and I don't even know his name."

"You're crazy!" She gave her a crooked smile, looking disappointed. "You're going to make a lot of people very unhappy. But, don't worry. I'll keep your secret."

Someone was calling her name, and she snapped back to reality, remembering she was at work. Then she saw Mrs. Adajian walking toward her. 'I was just thinking of her and here she is right in front of me. This is my lucky day.'

"Did you have a nice time at the dance, Virginia?"

"Yes, very nice. Did you?"

"Lovely. The Hotel Bond is such an amazing place and the music was just perfect."

"Um, Mrs. Adajian, um, who was that man sitting at your table? Is he a friend?"

"Yes, he is. He's a friend of our family."

She tried to sound nonchalant, "Really? Is he from this area?" As she shuffled merchandise from one side to another.

"Yes, he has a cleaning and tailoring shop on Sisson Avenue, just off Farmington Avenue."

"What's his name?"

"His name is George. George Avak."

"That's an unusual name. Is he Greek?" She silently prayed to God to make it true. "Does he have family around here?"

"He's Armenian. He changed his name from Avak Achjian to George Avak and he's here alone. We are his family now. When I first heard we had an Armenian tailor in Hartford, I went to see him. I walked in and I said, "inchpeses" which is hello in Armenian, he got up and rushed over to me and we shook hands. He was so happy to meet someone Armenian. Would you like to meet him?"

'Oh my God, how should I answer and not let her see I'm ready to faint.'

"That would be nice," trying to act nonchalant.

"Why don't you come to the Round Table tomorrow for lunch, and I'll invite him, too?" She looked at Virginia with her dancing eyes and a broad smile showing her perfect teeth.

"Oh, okay. That sounds nice."

"Shall we say around noon?"

"Yes, that would be fine." She was sure Mrs. Adajian could see her hands trembling.

Mrs. Adajian left the store and Virginia could feel herself shaking. 'Oh God, how am I going to do this? First thing, I have to do is tell Mr. Terwilliger that I'm going out for lunch tomorrow. Then, what am I going to wear? I'm never going to sleep tonight.'

Just then her friend Marianna walked in with her mother. Virginia went over, greeted them and asked how she could be of help. They were looking for material to make curtains for Marianna's new apartment. Her mother looked at her and said, "Virginia, I understand a proxinia is in the works for you, hum? How nice," With a sleek smirk slightly tilting her head, eyebrows raised.

Virginia didn't answer and just looked down. The mother laughed and walked away but

Marianna stayed behind and grabbed her by the arm. Looking at Marianna, Virginia could see marks on her face covered up with makeup. She thought, 'He must be hitting her too."

"Remember what I told you. Don't do it. Find your own husband."

After her encounters with Marianna at the dance and today, Virginia felt stronger than ever in her convictions.

She was very nervous about her luncheon with Mrs. Adajian and her prospective meeting with this Adonis.

'I just have to take a look at him and see where he works. I have to know a little more about him before I actually meet him.'

After work she took the trolley up Farmington Avenue. She had never been up this way before, but she was on a mission. She got off at Sisson Avenue. She walked by a drug store and continued to walk past a small grocery store, on her side of the street. Directly across the street was a large sign, "Sisson Avenue Cleaners and Dyers." Below the sign a picture window gave her a full view inside the store. 'Mm, he works by himself; he must own it.'

While she was staring at him, a tall, willowy woman came walking down the street toward the store. She was dressed in a white suit, very high heels and a large brimmed hat. Her figure reminded Virginia of an ironing board; long and slim. She tried not to be conspicuous and walked a little further down the street, still keeping her eye on the store, the woman and George. When the woman approached the store, she stopped, removed her hat and fluffed up her chestnut, shoulder length hair. She turned the knob and walked in, so confidently. George looked up from his seat and walked toward her. They shook hands and he gave her an affectionate, broad smile.

After searching through the rack, he found the woman's garment, covered it with a manila bag and handed it to her. She paid, and they shook hands again, but this time he clasped his left hand over hers and smiled. She smiled back very sweetly. Admiring herself in the floor mirror she slowly placed her hat gently back on her head. Turning to walk out the door she gave a slight hesitation, a half turn and a sheepish smile. Virginia got a glimpse of how beautiful she was. She noticed she had a very small nose. 'Why don't I have a very small nose like hers?' as she rubbed her fingers down her own nose. 'Why am I asking myself this question? I'm Greek. I have a Greek nose. Everything about me is Greek!' The woman, head held high, sporting a broad smile left the store.

George walked over and stood at the door watching her walk down the street, his hands on his hips. She must have known he was watching her because she turned slightly as she continued to walk and gave him a little wave at the same time.

'I wonder if he likes her. The exchange was too intimate.' A sense of alarm came over her. 'I feel sick to my stomach. I never should have come. Why did I? What have I done?'

Pacing back and forth in front of his store she had to think. 'What to do? What to do?'

She ran to the corner to catch the trolley home. Then she ran back and sat on the stoop in front of the drug store. She wrapped her arms around her legs to keep them from shaking, as she rocked back and forth, letting out little moans. 'How much of a chance am I going to have if he really likes her? Where is that going to leave me? I'm scared.' Panic was setting in. If he doesn't like me, John is going to make me marry Theodore to clear the way for Theresa. Oh God help me!'

She paced back and forth, again. Anxiety ripped at her while waiting for the trolley. When it finally arrived she got on and found a seat next to the window. She was fighting the urge to cry, taking a hanky from her pocketbook, dabbing her eyes and blowing her nose.

Just then a man came and sat next to her.

"Are you all right? Can I help you?"

"I'm fine."

"Would you like to talk?"

"No."

"Don't you remember me? I sold you the red dress. Did you have a good time at the dance?"

"Oh yes, I do remember you." Hiccupping. "You were so nice to have it ready for me," and then she started to really cry.

She felt vomit rising in her throat. She found herself gripping on to the metal bar on the seat in front of her while still keeping her head facing forward. 'I'm going to be sick.' Her trolley stop couldn't come soon enough.

"Why are you crying?"

"Oh, my brother is interfering with my life and I don't know what to do."

"Can I help?"

She shook her head, no, and blew her nose. "My brother wants me to marry someone I don't want to marry."

"I see, sort of a match making thing, huh?"

She nodded her head.

"Ah, you poor kid, be strong. If there is anything I can do to help you, I'll do it, anything at all. I'm available." He put his hand on hers and squeezed it, looking straight into her eyes.

'What did this mean?' She thanked him and her stop came just in time.

When she got out she ran to a large bush and threw up behind it, wiped her mouth with her hanky, then she felt a little better. She had to keep her misgivings in check. She stood up straight and walked determinedly home.

She wanted to be strong and confident and, concentrate on tomorrow and not fall apart.

She got home later than usual just as the sun was setting and dusk was approaching. As she came in through the front door, John got up from his chair and began giving her the third degree.

"Where were you? I was getting worried."

"I missed the trolley."

"How could you miss the trolley?"

"Are you worried because I got paid today and you weren't going to get your money? Here!" handing him her money envelope.

"You know perfectly well that's not the reason. I was just worried."

"Well, I'm home now. There's nothing to worry about."

She knew that by throwing guilt back at John he'd lay off, and it worked.

Just before dinner, Cynthia produced Virginia's journal. "What's this? I was changing the sheets and this fell on the floor."

"Oh, that's just a book from school."

"It's got an awful lot of writing in it. What does it say?"

John looked at the journal, waiting for her answer.

"It's from when I went to school. I like to look it over to refresh my memory."

She took it from her mother and flipped through it like it was just a notebook from school, not to throw suspicion her way. Her hands trembled. John said, "Let me have a look at that. Is there something I could learn?"

"I doubt that John, you know everything."

He grabbed it from her and flipped through the pages. What caught his eye was that it was all her writing.

"Tepsi, get my glasses. I want to read this."

"Sure, John."

Virginia's hands were trembling now and beads of sweat appeared on her forehead.

"I'll get your glasses for you, John." Virginia said.

Both girls got up and scurried around to find his glasses. Virginia found them and eyed Tepsi. Tepsi took the glasses and hid them underneath the sofa. Both girls went in different directions saying they couldn't find them.

Cynthia said. "Read it later. Dinner is ready, it's getting cold."

Virginia took the journal from John and flipped it on the chair far away from him and started to eat. For now, John's interest was averted. Theresa started talking about her job as a seamstress and John forgot all about the journal, for the moment.

CHAPTER 14

The Almost Meeting

She woke very early the next morning, washed her hair and curled it. Spring was definitely here and she felt it. She couldn't sleep with so many things to be concerned about. 'I'll wear my floral dress with the matching belt, showing off my figure, and my cream shoes.' Tepsi was watching her as she primped in front of the mirror.

"Do you think he's going to show up today, Ginger?"

"I hope so. Mrs. Adajian said she would invite him."

She bent over and kissed Tepsi on the cheek, whispering, "Wish me luck." Running out to catch the trolley she didn't want to tell Tepsi of her trepidation after witnessing the episode of the day before. She made it to work in plenty of time but couldn't concentrate on anything; the hands on the stubborn clock didn't seem to move. At 11:00 the phone rang and Mr. Terwilliger called to Virginia. The call was for her. She walked to the back of the store and he handed her the phone.

"Hi, Virginia. This is Pearl Adajian."

"Yes."

"I'm so sorry, honey. I'm going to have to cancel our luncheon date for today. I just realized I have another appointment. We'll make it another time. Maybe the end of the week, say Friday?"

"Yes, Friday sounds fine." Her disappointment reflected in her voice.

'Today was Tuesday and now I have to wait until Friday. Oh, God, I have to wait until Friday?'

The next day was Wednesday. Watching people out the front window of the store, she saw Mr. Gray approaching the store. She forgot all about this guy. He walked over to her and asked how she was feeling, handing her a tiny bouquet of violets.

"I'm feeling okay, thank you. Are these for me?"

"Yes. I thought maybe the flowers would cheer you up. Can we go for a walk?"

"Oh, I'm sorry I can't. I have too much work to do. But I thank you for the flowers."

"Maybe, another time, then? Don't forget to put the flowers in water."

"I won't, and thank you again."

She waved good-bye and gave him a smile, and walked to the back of the store.

'Don't I have enough troubles without adding one more?'

At 11:00 on Friday morning. The telephone rang and Mr. Terwilliger answered.

"Virginia. It's for you."

She took the phone with sweaty palms.

"Hello."

"Hi Virginia, it's Pearl Adajian.

"Oh yes. How are you?"

"Just fine, thank you. Is 12:00 today a good time for lunch?"

"Just a moment, I have to ask my boss."

He was standing right there and nodded.

"I guess it's okay." as nonchalant as she could muster.

"Wonderful. I'll see you at noon."

"Okay." She was afraid to get too excited after what happened the last time.

She ran to the trolley stop and waited, thinking. 'Is this really true? Am I actually going to meet him?' The trolley came and as she got on, the girls from work were watching her and waving. She could feel their anticipation. She got off right in front of the "Round Table Restaurant', checked her hair in her purse mirror and walked down the circular staircase into the restaurant. Mrs. Adajian was there to greet her. They exchanged pleasantries, and when she turned around there he was, standing right there next to her.

Mrs. Adajian said, "Virginia, I would like you to meet George and George, I would like you to meet Virginia."

"How do you do" he said, and with that he took her hand and kissed it. She thought she would faint. She could feel her heart pounding in her chest; and her face flushed and prickly. Could he see how nervous she was?' The tables were set for four with red and white checkered tablecloths on each one.

The three of them sat for lunch. Pearl kept the conversation going asking questions about her family. The food smelled so wonderful, but she didn't remember tasting a bite.

George explained how he worked in New York City and came to Connecticut to open his own business. The only relative he had was his uncle in

Canada. Pearl and her husband, Joe, had welcomed him into their lives.

"I've gone to many Armenian functions with them these past years. They are wonderful friends." He smiled at Pearl. He seemed to be enjoying his food while he spoke. "At the Bond, I noticed you dancing in your red dress and I told Pearl that I would like to meet you. Then, she told me she knew you. It was my good luck that she invited me to have lunch with you today."

"I noticed you too." He smiled and she could see his even teeth with just a little separation in between his two front ones. I'm so happy to have lunch with you and Mrs. Adajian."

"Please call me Pearl."

"I will. Thank you. But I do have to get back."

"Can I ride with you, Virginia?"

"Yes, I would love that."

When they walked out into the open air, it was as if her dreams were coming true; being doubly sure her feet were planted on the ground.

Waiting to cross the street to get the trolley, Virginia looked up and there was her brother's friend, Fred, from the pool hall, looking straight at her. She turned and faced the other direction, hoping he didn't see her. What would she ever say if Fred told John he saw her with a man?

George gently took her arm and crossed the street to get the trolley. Just his touch sent tingles through her spine. 'Was this a dream, or was this really happening?'

He asked if he could see her again. She explained about the proxinia.

"But do you have a ring?" He asked.

"No, I don't."

"Then there's a chance for me?"

"Of course there is. Next Saturday night we are going dancing at the pavilion. Would you like to meet us there?"

"It sounds wonderful. What time?"

"Is 7:30 okay?"

He took her arm and whispered, "I'll be there. I can't wait."

She got off the trolley and waved good-bye. When she got into work the girls were around her with questions, peering out the door to get a glimpse of him, at the same time.

"Oh my, he's gorgeous. Are you going to see him again?"

"He's going to meet us at the pavilion next Saturday." she squealed.

The chorus, "We wouldn't miss this."

"Time to get back to work girls," Mr. Terwilliger smiled laughingly.

CHAPTER 15

The Pavilion

"Dancing"

> On with the dance! Let joy be unconfined;
> No sleep till morn,
> When youth and pleasure meet.
>
> ~Byron "Childe Harold"

A few days went by before the meeting at the pavilion. 'I wonder if he'll show up. I wonder if I'm just imagining that he liked me. Maybe that's the way he acts with all the girls. What will I say to the girls if he doesn't show up? They're going to know I was jilted. What if he comes to the dance, and brings that girl from the store?"

'I wonder if he has match making in his country. I never asked him where he's from. I don't even know if he was ever married. Wouldn't John love that? Why is it men think they have control of the women in their family?'

She arrived at the pavilion as she had before; leaving Theresa as guard and climbing out the window and scaling down the side of the house; running – not to be late. At the steps of the dance floor her friends were waiting for her with big smiles. This was a big night, George might come.

Looking over to the other side of the pavilion, Virginia saw him, so tall, easy to identify. Coming closer she noticed he was alone! She kept staring at his face – wanting to entrench it to memory. 'Should she rush up to meet him or should she wait for him to come to her? I'll wait.' She decided.

She could feel her heart beat louder, the closer he came. 'He has such charisma!' She introduced him to her friends and with each one he shook hands, repeated her name and looked straight into her eyes. What seductive charm!

The music began, a foxtrot and George took her hand and they walked to the center of the floor, Virginia feeling everyone's eyes on her. 'I'm so glad I wore my dancing shoes and this fancy dress.' Right at this moment she felt her dreams were coming true. 'I can't believe this is actually happening to me.' She felt as if she could follow him anywhere.

"Where did you learn how to ballroom dance?" she asked.

"When I worked in New York City, on some Saturday nights the boys and I would go to the ballroom and dance. I'm so glad I did. Now, here I am dancing with you."

"Thank you."

Just for a fleeting moment, he remembered being fleeced.

The name of the song was "The Man I Love."

> Someday he'll come along, the man I love
> And he'll be big and strong, the man I love
> Hmmm I can make him mine.
> Maybe I will meet him someday, maybe
> Monday, maybe not.
> Hmmm Maybe Tuesday will be my good
> news day.
> We'll build a little nest, just made for two.
> And never more to roam, who would, would
> you?

'This song was written for me and for this night.'

After several dances, they met the others at the side of the Pavilion, and George bought them each a soda pop as the music died down. She and George danced some more, much closer this time, until it was the last dance.

They all walked along in a dreamy mood until they reached George's two - seater and the girls said their good-byes. George and Virginia lingered a while.

Virginia had to confess, "You know, George, my family doesn't know I'm out. I have to rush back before they discover I'm missing."

"You mean you can't even go out with your friends?"

"No. My brother is very strict."

"I'll drive you home."

"Oh no, I'll run home it's just a short way."

"When will I see you again?"

"I don't know."

"I'll come by the S&A tomorrow. We'll talk."

"Okay." She said running toward the Avenue, aware of his gaze.

CHAPTER 16

George's Pursuit

George couldn't get Virginia out of his mind. That's all he thought about. He closed the store and drove to the Round Table to see Pearl.

"Pearl, you have to help me."

"What? How can I lend a hand?"

'Well, I'm really interested in Virginia. There is someone she's supposed to marry, but I know she isn't interested in him. The family is trying to match her up."

"How do you know that?"

"Because I can tell she likes me."

"Well, what is it you like about her? I have introduced you to so many Armenian girls and you have never said that about any one of them."

"She makes me feel good. She makes me happy. She looks at life as fun. She loves music, and when she hears it she lights up. She has a special magic. I have been with so many sad girls. I just want to be with someone who's happy and wants a happy life. When I first came to this country I was lost and afraid. But living here I have found the opportunity to control and determine my own life, I want to do all that with her. I have to buy her a ring, so she and her family know I have honorable intentions."

"You just can't go and buy her a ring, George. You have to pursue her and go out with her and date her."

"But her family will not allow it."

"Then you'll just have to find another way."

"I'm going to go and wait for her after work. We'll map out a plan and then I'll ask her to marry me. If she says yes, then we'll go directly to her family and tell them. What can they do if she has a ring? Throw me out? At least I will have given her a ring. This other fellow hasn't given her the respect she deserves. Maybe he realizes she doesn't really care for him and that's why the hesitation."

"But George, how can you be so sure she cares for you?"

"I can tell. I know she's very interested in me. I can tell by the way she looks at me and the way she responds when I touch her. She's full of fun and laughs a lot. I'm happy when I'm around her. I just want to be with her."

"But her family, they only want their girls to marry someone Greek."

"I can be Greek. I speak a little Greek and I'm ready to become part of her Greek family. I can even cook Greek."

Then they both laughed.

"Okay, honey, good luck. But wait before you buy the ring."

"No, I'm buying the ring. I'll just hold on to it for a while."

CHAPTER 17

"Your Laughter"

"Take bread away from me, if you wish, take air away, but do not take from me your laughter."
~Pablo Neruda

George was ready to take the plunge, a little like stepping on to a frozen lake, unsure if it would support him. He drove to the S&A at 4:45. He parked the car. Trembling he walked into the store. Virginia looked up and saw him standing there.

"My, it's wonderful to see you."

"I'll wait for you to get off of work."

"I have another ten minutes."

"That's okay. I can wait."

160

Mr. Terwilliger looked over and saw George and waved to him and yelled to Virginia,

"It's okay. You can go, Virginia." He mouthed, with a sly smile.

"Thank you very much. See you tomorrow." Grabbing her purse.

She was so nervous, her hands were trembling but she held them tightly squeezing her fingers together to stop them from shaking.

"I'd like to ride with you on the trolley."

"Okay," trying to keep her voice calm.

She wondered if she was doing the right thing. They waited for the trolley in silence. She looked around to see if anyone she knew was watching them. He let her get on first then they took their seats. When they sat, he took her hand. Virginia gave him a quizzical look, not knowing what to expect.

"I have a question I want to ask you."

"You do?"

"Yes."

George turned to her. "Virginia, I am Armenian. I have no family. But I have a good business and I do quite well. I can support you so you will never have to work. I know your family wants you to marry a Greek, but I can become Greek. I think

161

about you all the time and, I would like for us to get to know each other."

"I want to be with you, too."

"Virginia, I know your family doesn't allow dating. But I want to see you more and more. You're not actually betrothed."

"No, but my mother and brother won't allow me to date."

"We don't have to tell them."

Right there Virginia felt ambivalence. She couldn't pass up this opportunity, but she would be deceiving her family. She found herself spellbound, looking into his eyes and said, "Yes, we don't have to tell them."

"We're not doing anything wrong. We're just taking the trolley together, right?"

She smiled and took a deep breath, still feeling deceitful. He kept talking and telling her of his plans to marry and settle down, buy a home and have children. She just listened. By the time the ride came to her stop, he had convinced her that this was their only choice.

Virginia felt her lips quiver.

"I knew the minute I saw you that you were the one for me. I just knew it." She said.

"And I fell in love with you the moment I saw you in that red dress. Would it be okay if I come to get you tomorrow, too?"

For the next two weeks George came to get Virginia and took the ride home on the trolley. They talked and talked about their hopes and dreams for the future; they seemed to have so much to say. However, George never told her the details of his beginnings, just that he lost his family in Turkey. Virginia told him about her father, and how difficult it was to grow up in a new country without a father and no money.

In the meanwhile her family kept insisting that she go through with the proxy. She kept very quiet and rarely registered her opinion, waiting until she had a plan. To argue at this point was fruitless. 'It's going to be very difficult to convince them that she already has a beau; and someone of whom they would disapprove.'

Their plan was that they would meet at the park and take a walk, and if the band was there they would dance. She would sneak out of her room at night by climbing out the window, shimmying down the side of the house and making a run for it – her usual escape. They spent a little time together before it was time for her to rush back home.

One night, the moon was bright and the stars shown aglow. It was as if street lights were not a necessity. Virginia ran her usual routine; climbing out the window, shimmying down the side of the house and running to the park. Waiting for the right moment to cross the street, Virginia saw John's two-seater cruising down the street.

"Oh My God!" Trembling with fear, she crouched down behind a parked car.

'What if he saw me? What am I going to say? I know, I'll just deny it was me.' But all that evening she worried. George could see the change in her. When she told him what had happened, George made up his mind right then. He was now going to make his move.

The next day George showed up after work with his car.

"We're not taking the trolley?"

He opened the passenger door for her to get it and went around to the driver's side and got in.

"Let's take a little ride before we go to your house."

"But you don't know where I live."

"You'll show me."

They went for a drive up through the grounds of Trinity College and parked the car.

He looked squarely into her eyes, taking her hands into his.

"Virginia, these past two weeks have been the happiest in my life. I want to spend the rest of my life with you. Will you do me the honor of marrying me?"

She closed her eyes and took a deep breath and nodded, yes. Then she said,

"But we have a very big problem with my family."

"I know, I know. I have the answer. Keep your eyes closed."

He took the ring from the box and placed it on her finger. She didn't even have to look at it, because even if it were a band from a cigar, she would cherish it forever. They kissed very passionately and, she ran her fingers through his gorgeous hair.

After such passion, Virginia couldn't remember where she was. She looked around in a daze. "Where am I?" When she acclimated herself, she whispered, "What are we going to do about my family?"

"We're going to your house right now, and tell them we are going to be married. Once they see the ring on your finger they will approve. I just know it."

CHAPTER 18

"When I found you, I found me"
~Jeff Pitchell

Virginia and George pulled up in front of the house about 6:00. She was late and she knew John would be worried.

"Where could she be? This is the second time she's been late from work. I wonder what's going on with her?"

"Stop worrying, John. She'll be here," Theresa said, trying to calm him.

John looked out the window and saw Virginia and George getting out of his car and walking up the sidewalk. It was a brisk evening and heavy clouds hung from the sky. George held her hand tightly keeping steady from the force of the wind.

"Oh no, oh my God, she's coming up the walk with a man holding her hand."

John stood in the doorway, hands in his pockets. Theresa ran out the front door to greet them. The rest of the family, in shock, stayed in the parlor.

"Look, look, Tepsi, look what I've got. This is George, and he proposed to me. We're going to be married."

Theresa jumped up and kissed George as he picked her up and kissed her back. She was so little it didn't take much strength. She took Virginia's hand and walked them into the house, beaming with delight.

"Look, look. Virginia has a diamond. Virginia has a diamond." Her mother came from the kitchen wiping her hands on her apron.

Virginia and George looked at John first, and then her mother. There was complete silence. George walked over to John and extended his hand. John had no recourse but to oblige.

"I want to marry Virginia. May I sit down?"

No one answered but he sat anyway and pulled Virginia down with him.

"We have been taking the trolley together and gotten to know each other and we have decided we want to be married. Virginia has told me that you want her to marry someone Greek. I know that, but we love each other. I have my own business and I can support her. I have no family and I want to become part of yours. I consider myself Greek already." He said smiling opening up his arms, confident that his speech had won them over.

John had a skeptical look and nodded his head. "We know nothing about you. Where are you from and what do you want with my sister?"

"What I want with you sister is to make her my wife. We love each other, and I promise you, I will make her happy. I will become part of your family. Trust me."

Virginia looked at John with an appealing expression, hoping for his approval, waiting for an answer, but none came. Virginia called Dorothy and invited her and her family to come over, even though John was showing his disapproval. As the evening progressed, Virginia could see John sizing up George. 'He's probably thinking, 'how can I find a way to sponge off of him, too!'

To Virginia's surprise, the family was cordial, even though they were disappointed.

"You know there is a Greek interested in my sister. His name is Theodore," John said.

"Yes, I know that; but I have given her a ring and she has accepted."

Virginia knew this wasn't going to be easy; but did John have to be so obvious?

"Don't worry about the expense of a wedding. My friend Pearl Adajian and I will take care of everything," assured George. My uncle is a priest and he will marry us if that's okay with you."

Virginia thought that would appease the family but it didn't. They were all angry except for Theresa, who held back not to contradict John.

"Well, if Mrs. Adajian is willing, then go right ahead and make your plans. You know we don't have much money."

"There goes John and his negativity." Virginia whispered to Theresa.

"Pearl and I will take care of everything. Don't worry."

John offered more coffee, but Virginia could see he was seething.

After George left, no one spoke to her. No one offered congratulations or said they were happy for her. 'That's okay, I don't care. If that's the way they want to be, so be it.'

She went to her room and wrote about the whole night in her journal. Somehow by writing and reliving it, she realized that she had made the right decision. She wanted to be with George no matter what the consequences. And, there were going to be many consequences.

The next morning Virginia couldn't wait to get to work and show the girls her diamond.

"Do you notice anything different about me?"

"No. Not really."

Virginia waved her left hand in front of them.

"Ah," they screamed in unison, gathering around to admire her ring.

"Congratulations," rang through the store. "When are you getting married?"

"I have no idea, one step at a time!"

She never let on about the turmoil going on at home.

Very late in the day, Virginia was taking merchandise out of boxes and putting it on the shelves. When she looked up, she saw Dorothy standing at the end of the counter.

"Hi, Dorothy. What brings you into town?"

"I've come here to talk to you."

"Oh, what can I do for you?"

"I've come to tell you that Jack and I will not be coming to your wedding."

"Oh, I see." Her mouth dropped.

"You are making the whole family very upset. You are ruining your life."

"Let me be the judge of that. Dorothy, do you remember your proxinia and I questioned you? You said, "Can't you be happy for me? And I said, "If you're happy, I'm happy. Can't you do that for me?"

"You're breaking all the traditions by marrying George. You know that. So, none of us will be coming to the wedding."

"I'm sorry you feel that way. You've made your choice and I've made mine."

She turned and walked to the back of the store to attend to a customer and never looked back.

When George picked her up from work, she told him what had transpired.

"Has this encounter, with your sister, changed your mind?"

"Never!" She grabbed him, put her arms around his neck and kissed him on the cheek. "Never!"

Driving home he said Pearl was making a dress and a veil for her. It's going to be a big surprise.

"You mean it?"

"Ah- ha."

Now she was excited again.

"I think we should marry soon. Your family is going to make it very difficult for you during this time; how about next Sunday?"

"It sounds heavenly to me."

CHAPTER 19

The Wedding

"Always"

Bring them all where I wait for you: we shall always be alone, we shall always be, you and I, alone upon the earth to begin life.

~Pablo Neruda

The day before the wedding Virginia placed her tattered valise on her bed. She was invited to spend her last single night at the Adajian's home. Pearl had sewn her dress and made all the wedding plans, so it was only fitting for her to be there, too.

The first thing she put in the valise was her journal, then her red dress. After that it didn't matter what she threw in. The door opened. Virginia turned around to see her mother, sad and desperate. She came into the bedroom and closed the door behind her. She sat on the corner of the bed and patted her hand on the bedspread for Virginia to sit next to her.

"This decision you have made is breaking my heart. Not only because I wanted you to marry Greek, but that you don't even know this man. We don't know from where he comes, we don't know about his family, we don't know anything. I worry for your future. I worry that he won't make you happy."

"I'm very happy, Mother. Don't worry about me. I have been in love with this man even before I met him. That my family won't be at the wedding is your choice, not mine," and she kept packing.

Her mother looked down and whispered, "It's not my choice. It's your brother's."

She got up from the bed and stroked her daughter's hair. "You are always with me, my Virginia. You are different from Dorothy and Theresa. You always had a spirit about you struggling to conform. That you are doing this, is not a total surprise to me. You've always had your own ideas. I pray for you and I will always love you, no matter what. You always have me beside you."

"I know Mom. You are always in my heart too. I love you and admire you for all the anguish you've been through and all that you've done for me. But now it's my turn to make my way with the man I love. I know you want the best for me. This is what's best for me." Her mother kissed her affectionately, but Virginia could tell she was torn.

"Mom, I know you want to be happy for me. I hope in time you will love George, too."

Virginia knew that in choosing this path over another there would be no going back.

In her eyes this was the most beautiful wedding. She felt like a princess in the magnificent dress Pearl had made of pure silk chiffon; long sleeves and a V neck. She carried two dozen white roses with streamers ending with stephanotis. Pearl and Joe stood up for them. Joe and George were in black tuxedos and Pearl wore a grey chiffon dress. The classical music, playing in the background calmed Virginia; leaving all negative thoughts behind. Their restaurant made all the Armenian refreshments, elegantly presented. Virginia found herself peering at the front door, hoping her family would change their minds. She couldn't believe that they were actually going to go through with their promise. It was so sad for her that they didn't come. 'It's okay if my family won't talk to me. It was not a Greek Orthodox ceremony. It was an Armenian Orthodox ceremony. It was pretty close, and it didn't matter to me.'

George looked at Virginia after the ceremony and sighed "I've never been happier in my life than today." And Virginia looked into his warm dark eyes and thought, 'My life begins right at this moment.'

Father Devletian sat with Virginia and told her of their time in Marseille, and of George's plight. She could hardly believe that he had actually witnessed his family's slaughter. He told her to expect moments of sadness, which most Armenians go through. But what George witnessed, is something he will never completely overcome. She felt a lump in her throat and fear for what may come.

There was no honeymoon. Virginia brought her suitcase to George's apartment next door to his shop. Later they moved to a larger apartment, on South Whitney Street, when Virginia got pregnant. George was so happy. He came home for lunch every day to check on her.

"Are you all right? Do you feel okay?"

"I'm fine. I'm fine."

But during her first trimester she lost the baby. When George got home from work he found her doubled over with pain and crying.

"I'm being punished. My family isn't talking to me and now I lost our baby."

"Now, now, Ginger, you're talking nonsense, stop being foolish. We'll try again. Just rest and I'll take care of you. Here put your head on me." as he stroked her hair.

He put his arms around her and told her how much he loved her. "Our lives will only get better, you'll see." He was right. After a few months' time she became pregnant again.

However, this time, she lost the baby again. They became very depressed and worried that they were under some kind of a curse. The doctor suggested she get her strength back before getting pregnant again.

When she was 29 years old, she became pregnant for the third time. This time the doctor wanted her to have bed rest and no exertion. After three months the doctor was certain she would hold the baby, and she did.

On November 6, 1932 Virginia awoke with labor pains.

"George, wake up. I think I'm having the baby."

"What? Are you sure?"

"George, I mean it. I'm having a tightening feeling in my stomach and then, it stops. I think this is what they said happens."

George got out of bed and began pacing the floor. "Maybe you'd better pace the floor with me."

He helped her put on her slippers and they both walked around the apartment. After a few minutes she let out a yelp and a scream then doubled over.

"I think I'd better call the doctor."

"I think so too, ouch."

"How often are the pains?" the doctor asked.

"I would say often."

"Keep track and we'll be right there."

The doctor came with his nurse and midwife with all their paraphernalia for the delivery. The pains were now every two minutes and George was distraught. The doctor didn't know who to tend to first: George or Virginia.

"Okay, George. Leave the room. I'll take over from here."

"Okay, I'll be right here in the hallway."

They prepared in a hurry because now the contractions were getting very close. Listening to Virginia scream in agony, George was wringing his hands and soaked in perspiration. Her screams were reminiscent of his mother's screams. Then he began to think 'Oh my God. What if I lose my wife? What if she dies? I hear some women lose their life while giving birth.' When George heard the baby cry, he bolted to the door and opened it. He looked at Virginia and saw blood on the sheets and fell to the floor in a heap.

"Oh my god, get the smelling salts in my bag. Break it and put it under his nose. There's no time for this, George. The midwife is tending to your wife, and the nurse and I are tending the baby. Wake up, Wake up." They sat him upright on the floor out in the hall and ordered him to stay there. "We're not ready for you.

He continued screaming "My wife my wife. Virginia, are you okay?"

"Just stay in the hallway, George, and wait for the doctor to call you, okay?"

"Okay. The baby, is the baby okay?"

"The baby is fine. Go into the hallway."

The doctor turned to him and said, "Go into the hallway. You have a son."

"I have a son? Oh my God. We have a son."

Sitting on the floor, his elbows resting on his knees, he buried his head in his hands and cried and cried. 'My wife didn't die, and I have a son."

Completely exhausted, he went into the bathroom and washed his face and hands and put on a clean shirt.

"Okay George, we're ready for you." called the nurse.

He came into their bedroom, sunlight leaping into the room through their large windows. Virginia was sitting up, in a pink flowered bed jacket, holding their son. He walked over to them, kissed his wife and looked at his son. Oh my god, he's beautiful, counting his fingers and toes.

"Dr. Zariphes says that he's at least ten pounds. I was so worried about handling a new born but not now; I don't think he'll break. He looks very sturdy."

With curly black hair and big black eyes, he was the mirror image of his daddy with a look of determination.

After the doctor, midwife and his nurse left, George wanted to call John and tell him that the baby had arrived. He didn't want to tell Virginia just in case no one came. He made the call to John, and said they had a son. He wondered if this would break the ice and they would finally become a family. Well it did. The next day George put a closed sign on the door to spend the day with his "family." John brought Cynthia and Theresa to meet Virginia and George's son. While the women were in with the baby, John asked George if he could talk to him.

"Sure, John, what can I do for you?"

"Well, can we step outside?"

"Sure, let me get my coat."

They walked outside and down the steps from the house and strolled along the sidewalk. The air was brisk and clear. What a day to be a daddy! George thought.

"How are you doing, George? I mean financially?"

"What?"

"I mean, how are you doing financially?"

"My business is doing very well, and I'm close to having enough money to buy a home." George answered confused.

"Well, I was wondering, George. Do you think you could lend me some money?"

"Why, is there some trouble?"

No, no, it's just that we have a match for Theresa and she'll be leaving. Her job at the materials factory helped a lot but, now her money will be going to her husband."

"I don't understand the problem, John."

"The problem is there's going to be less money coming into the house and I have to take care of Mom."

George turned and faced him, putting his hands on his shoulders.

"Look John, I will always help you when there is a need. I think you need to get a job. You can no longer hang out at the pool hall and the coffee houses. If I give you money, that's where you'll spend it. You like to drive. There are plenty of businesses on Franklin Avenue who need drivers. As a matter of fact, there's a coffee business owned by Greeks on Franklin Avenue. Why don't you go there and ask if they need any help?"

John, feeling rejected and embarrassed at the same time, took George's hands away from his shoulders, nodded and started to amble back into the house.

Pondering his suggestion, John said, "Maybe I'll give it a try."

"Good man."

There's something about a baby that removes all animosity. Virginia's family did come more frequently to see this beautiful baby, who was part of all of them. With reservation John seemed tolerant. But as time passed, John brought mother more frequently and they would have supper together. Cynthia loved to feed little George, and John loved to play with him. Little by little the fences were mending.

The Adajian family accepted Virginia as one of their own. The Avak's were invited to their home every Sunday. She loved going there and sitting at their large mahogany dining room table and eating Armenian food. She loved all their oriental carpets – so colorful and thick. Pearl was her friend. She became part of their family in the way she had hoped George would become part of hers.

"One Sunday while Pearl and Virginia were preparing dinner, George and Joe went downstairs to the finished basement to listen to Armenian and Turkish music on the phonograph. She noticed that Pearl became very quiet. Her bright eyes welled with tears. She took Virginia's hand and slowly, together, they went down stairs. George and

Joe were dancing to Turkish music and crying. When the music stopped the women walked over to them and no one said a word.

"Come, Joe, come, George it's over now. Come upstairs." Pearl coaxed.

Slowly they climbed the stairs still embracing. Dinner was very somber. Memories were flying all over the room. Virginia was worried."

Pearl explained to her that she thought it was cathartic for them to remember their loved ones while dancing the dance that had been passed down for generations.

The men retired to the living room and exchanged stories, speaking in Armenian.

'They understood each other. Who better to share George's grief?'

The ride home from the Adajian's was serene and peaceful. He tussled little George's hair and then took Virginia's hand; this gesture assured her that he was okay; ready to put it to rest, until the next time.

After living in an apartment for three years, they bought a home in West Hartford and the property next to it, and began to become part of a community. They were Greek and Armenian, not your typical family on their street of mostly Irish, Polish, Italian and French; again, another challenge.

After Virginia had spent the whole day rearranging furniture and hanging freshly starched cream colored curtains, George came home from work earlier than usual. He walked in and gave Virginia a big hug and a tender kiss.

She gently broke away and gestured with her hand as if making a presentation.

"Look George, look this is our home," Very proud of her efforts.

He took her into his arms again, delicately and whispered,

"You're my home."

"I love you, George, I'm so happy." They kissed again more passionately.

One by one, the neighbors came with cakes and cookies to welcome them into the neighborhood. They felt accepted and wanted. 'This is going to work out.' Virginia thought.

Soon Virginia became part of the neighborhood bridge group, coffee klatches and recipe exchanges. In the evening when the men came home from work, they visited at each other's backyards and exchanged household problems and solutions. George and Virginia had outgoing personalities that drew people to them.

One day the ladies decided to have a pot luck heritage night. Italian, Greek, Scot, Polish, Irish and French dishes were sampled. What a night they had.

"Gee, that was fun tonight."

"It was a good choice to move here don't you think, Virginia?"

"You're right. You're always right."

George let out a big laugh. "You're teasing me right?"

"Sort of."

CHAPTER 20

Finding Their Place

In time they had two children and a dog. Life was good, but difficult. There were times, as his uncle had warned, when George went into a pensive mood and became very sad. But when he watched the children play, and their daughter climbed on his knee, he was so happy.

When World War 11 broke out, no one was more patriotic than George. He organized the neighborhood to plant victory gardens. They compared the size and taste of each other's vegetables, and had picnics in their backyards, enjoying the fruits of their labor. Mrs. Casabella had the best recipe for fried squash flowers. Virginia made her cold cucumber soup. Mrs. Pulski made gilumpkies. Each came from a different country, spoke with a variety of accents, but all spoke English, even though it was broken.

There were only American flags waving from their porches. There were no Greek, Italian, Irish, Polish flags; they were Americans. While the adults were enjoying their food, the kids pretended to be soldiers marching in a parade. They put sticks over their shoulders, and sang as they marched:

> "Whistle while you work.
> Hitler is a jerk.
> Mussolini is a Meany.
> But the Japs are worse."

Even the children, as young as five years old knew the seriousness of the war. They listened, along with their parents, as President Roosevelt reported on the progress of the war and promoted War Bonds.

Both George and Virginia worried about Dorothy's son Louis who was in the Army. He was wounded and came home to recover, only to be redeployed.

Many times Virginia would bring their young daughter to the tailor shop to visit daddy. When she opened the front door to the shop their daughter would rush in screaming,

"Daddy. Daddy. Daddy," arms outstretched.

She'd giggle with glee as he picked her up and twirled her around. Virginia watched as her memory returned to her days as a child when her daddy would pick her up and twirl her around. Something very minute could bring back tender memories. Just from the look on George's face she could see how happy and complete he was. She brought him more joy than anyone else ever could.

George bought dark window shades for "black out" nights. They lived near a munitions factory, so when the strobe lights came on and the whistle blew he knew it was time to pull the shades for air raid drills. Nylon was reserved for making parachutes, so nylon was rationed. Butter, coffee, meat and sugar were also rationed. No one complained. They felt they were doing their part for the boys overseas.

George's backyard was his domain. His house was a three bedroom colonial with an attached garage. The quince tree produced fruit for jam. The apple tree produced fruit for pies. The weeping willow provided shade. The outdoor fireplace John and George built was perfect for shish-ka-bob. The cherry tree provided fruit for the birds. The fig tree provided figs for peeling and eating.

The day was winding down and the sunlight was diminishing toward dusk. "Virginia, come here and join me. It's such a beautiful night. Come and see how nice the yard looks."

She joined him on the lawn chair next to him and they had a quiet moment together.

"Life is good isn't it?"

"Life is good."

Even after so many years of marriage, she still looked at him with adoration. She knew she made the right choice no matter how challenging the obstacles. She wouldn't have changed a moment in her life.

George participated in every holiday, even Halloween.

"Come on kids. It's Halloween. Let's get dressed up and go trick or treating."

"You're kidding Dad."

"No I'm not. Virginia, let's go upstairs and find something for me to wear."

Within twenty minutes he came downstairs in a housedress, shoes with red bows, lipstick, rouge, earrings and a handbag. Virginia and the kids were doubled over with laughter. Now they were ready to 'trick or treat.'

The neighbors were hanging out their doors waiting for them to come up the street so they could have a good laugh, too.

George and his kids took paper bags and went up and down the street. The neighbors all loved it.

"Hey, George, come on over here, we're bobbing for apples. Try your luck!" The neighbors never forgot it.

He was an American and could do whatever he wanted and no one was going to interfere with the way he felt and his way of life.

However, his moments of hatred for the Turks would crop up now and then. One day as he worked alone at his store, a customer came in to have some trousers altered. He greeted George in Turkish.

"Are you Turkish?" George blurted out.

"Yes, I am."

George saw red. He lunged at him and grabbed his shirt with both fists.

"Get out! Get out!"

He threw the man outside, and he landed on the sidewalk, torn trousers and all.

"If you ever come here again, I'll kill you."

The man got up and went after George, goading him to continue the fight. They started punching each other in front of the store. People were stopped in their wake and a policeman came running.

"Break it up. Break it up." Officer O'Reilly pleaded.

"George, what are you doing? Stop, stop."

He pulled them apart. Each of them panting and trying to catch his breath; both of them were bleeding. Just then a cruiser pulled up and Officer O'Reilly put both of them into the car.

"Tell us what happened."

At that moment, George realized he didn't have a leg to stand on. When the man told his side of the story, the policeman asked if he wanted to press charges. He said no, he just wanted to go home. The second policeman walked him to the corner and made sure he wasn't terribly injured. Officer O'Reilly took George back into his store.

"Now, listen, George. You can choose who you want as customers and who you don't. However, you cannot raise a hand to them. Do you understand me? Otherwise you will land in jail; and I don't think you want that, do you?"

"No, Sir." George whispered with his head bent.

"I would miss our morning coffees together and our great discussions. I understand how you feel, but you have to let it go, George. You don't want these flare-ups to ruin your life."

After the officer left, George was totally humiliated. He was embarrassed that his associate businessmen had witnessed this; he felt ashamed. Nothing like this had ever happened before. 'I am in this wonderful country where I am secure; now I have to find security within myself.'

Joe, the next door shoemaker, had witnessed the whole episode and came into the store and patted him on the shoulder, "Go home, George. My wife is with me. She can watch my store, and I'll stay here until closing time to watch yours. Go home. Be with your family."

George thanked him and his eyes filled with tears. He arose from his chair, put his arms around Joe and let it all out and cried.

When he came through the door, very early, he told Virginia of the encounter and while she understood, she was frightened.

"George, look at all we have! Are you going to let one person, who comes into the store, spoil your life? You're the first one to say how grateful you are for all this country has offered to us. Why do you let this make you so angry?"

"You're right. I am trying. I'm telling you, I'm really trying, Virginia."

CHAPTER 21

A Special Person Comes To Call

One afternoon George called Virginia and said,

"You don't have to cook tonight. A new customer came into the store and she has invited us to dinner."

"You're kidding. Who is it?"

"She's Greek and she's from Smyrna. Guess what? She lives near us."

Virginia was surprised. "She wants us to come for dinner? Did you tell her we have two children?"

"She invited them, too. She said to be there at 6:00."

"Okay" she said taken aback. "We'll be ready."

The four of them arrived at her home at 6:00. It was a colonial house, painted dark green with black shutters. Virginia brought some homemade cookies and they rang the bell.

"Come in, come in. I'm Thana and this is my husband, Michael."

"Hi. This is my wife, Virginia, and our children."

They were very Greek but spoke English perfectly. Thana was caught up in the Turkish rampage of Smyrna in 1915. They raped, burned homes and destroyed everything in sight. The Greeks and Armenians couldn't get out fast enough. She told harrowing stories of being separated from her family and searching for them in a row boat. She never could find her mother and father, only her sister who was affected by the trauma for the rest of her life. Little row boats were heading toward large vessels which would rescue them if they could reach the ships.

Thana's eyes were sparkling silver as she related her story,

French, English and American ships were waiting for survivors in international waters. Woodrow Wilson was not willing to step in. He said, 'It's not our war.' But the American ships could not leave without trying to rescue whoever was approaching."

194

She went on. "I bless the American sailors who didn't leave me behind. I did hurt my leg getting onto the ship and no one tended to it, so consequently I walk with this limp. When I came to Connecticut I met Michael. His family had settled here much earlier and he was already an American citizen. I received my Master's Degree from Trinity College, and have been a social worker in Hartford for three years now."

George loved to listen to her speak; her story was so similar to his. They had an immediate bond, having suffered at the hands of the Turks.

"How about on Sunday Michael and I pick you up, and take you to church? Then you can meet some young couples your age and make some friends."

"That sounds wonderful," Virginia answered hopefully.

When they got back home, George told Virginia, 'You go to church on Sunday I'll stay home with the children."

"You mean you won't go with me?"

"No, you go ahead. Let me know how it was."

Here was another challenge for Virginia. She wondered why, but decided not to ask right then. 'I'll wait for the opportune moment to find out what's on his mind.'

That night when George went to bed his thoughts went to his friend Elizabeth from Smyrna. He wondered about her, and always planned to find out what happened to her.

Thana and Michael came on Sunday to pick them up.

"Where are George and the children?"

"He decided to stay home and take care of them rather than coming to Church."

"I wanted both of you to meet people at church. He isn't interested?"

"I think he blames God for what happened to his family. He suffers greatly because of that."

"I understand. But we all need to belong to a community. We need people around us to care for us in bad and in good times. I think I'll have a talk with him and see if I can change his mind. After all, this is for all of you."

Walking into the church Virginia felt a sense of homecoming. The smell of incense and the leaded glass icons on the windows were so familiar to her. She felt a surge of joy; as if she were home. I wonder what's on George's mind not wanting to come. Our children aren't going to grow up with God and have a religion? This is another mountain to climb but I'll worry about that later.

The service was two hours long and all in Greek. Of course he didn't want to come. He doesn't understand Greek that well and there weren't any translation books. Maybe it was better that he stayed home. Just before the communion offering, the congregation kneels and the choir sings 'se imnumen, thank you Jesus for your blessing.' Virginia knelt and prayed to God to keep her children healthy. Help George accept what happened to him in his childhood. Show him the way to love life and celebrate the blessings we have.

Periodically, Thana would visit George at the store and bring some Greek pastries and a thermos of coffee. They sat together and she tried to convince him that he needed church friends. She gave a pretty convincing argument. One day she and Michael came to their house for a visit.

Thana asked, "What are your plans to baptize the children?"

"I really hadn't thought about it much." George said.

"We do have to think about it, George." Virginia agreed.

"When you decide, Michael and I would love to become godparents to your children."

George was so attached to Thana and Michael he didn't hesitate. They had no children of their own.

"I can contact my uncle, who married us, he's in Canada. I can invite him to come and perform the ceremony and we can do it in the Greek Church."

This would become the beginning of their involvement in the church as they became associated with that community.

CHAPTER 22

A Proud Dad

George's most prideful moment was the day he took his son to college. He emptied the car of his son, Georgie's, belongings and the family walked to his dorm to find his room. They walked around the quad and marveled at the large buildings. When Georgie saw some boys going up to his dorm he said,

"Okay, Mom and Dad, it's time for me to go meet the guys." He was rooming with some of his high school buddies.

He gave each of them a hug. George forced back his tears, his heart filled with pride.

"Be good, son. If you need anything just let us know. Just call us any time, we would love to hear your voice."

"Sure thing, Dad, and thanks for everything."

"Call every week now," his mother echoed.

On the two hour drive home he held Virginia's hand smiling with a sense of accomplishment.

"We did it, one down and one more to go, right, honey?" turning around smiling at his daughter.

He was proud of his daughter, too. He loved listening to her practice her piano. He was so proud of her scholarship award for voice. Oh the joy he felt when he heard her sing! She was asked to sing a solo at a school talent show. They couldn't wait to go to hear her sing in front of an audience all by herself. He whipped up a black velvet dress with a lace collar for her to wear. All dressed in their finery they went to hear her sing.

When she was finished with her song the applause wouldn't stop. The audience kept clapping and clapping. Their daughter became overwhelmed by the audience's reaction. Only later would she understand that it was her father who wouldn't stop clapping, and kept the audience going.

CHAPTER 23

*"I think the purpose in life is to be useful, to be
responsible, to be honorable, to be compassionate. It
is, after all, to matter: to count, to stand for
something, to have made a difference that you lived
at all."*

~Leo Rosten

January 20, 1953 was a cold, snowy night.
Heavy snow flakes were swirling inhibiting
visibility. George closed the store early and stopped
by the gas station to have chains put on his tires.
Listening to Kate Smith finishing her program with
"God Bless America", he was concerned watching
the snow, through the lamp light, hitting the trees.

"Okay, Mr. Avak , you're good to go. Be careful
out there."

"Sure will. Thanks a lot, Joe."

"Say, Mr. Avak, how's your son doing in college?"

"He's doing great. He called us last night to tell us that he's now writing for his college newspaper. He loves it."

"Gee, that's great. How's your daughter doing?"

"She's doing well, too. She just received a vocal scholarship from Hartt School. We were thrilled about that because that's what she wants to do, and I certainly couldn't afford to pay for lessons."

"Well, good luck with everyone. Sounds like the gods are shining upon you. Say hello to Mrs. Avak for me, and be careful on the ride home."

"Sure will, thanks, Joe."

He was careful. Cars without chains were slipping all over the road. He couldn't help but notice how majestic the night was, though. The snow performed a ballet as the white dust blew above, accompanied by the music on his car radio. Executing the left turn on to his street, he did a 180. 'Ah, that was scary.' The rest of the ride to his house was downhill so he put the car in low gear. The garage door was left open for him. He made it up the driveway and into the garage without much difficulty. He came in through the garage door and was greeted by Virginia, his daughter, Gloria, and their dog Tiny. Virginia, in her apron, had the dinner ready and their daughter had just finished her homework.

"Boy, it's a rough night out there. I was lucky to get home. Cars were sliding all over the road." Feeling a great sense of relief he closed the door with the back of his heel and placed his grocery bag on the counter.

"Do you have anything for me Daddy?"

"Of course, I have a surprise for you."

Before taking off his coat, he reached into the bag and presented her with a package of Genoa salami.

"My favorite, can I have some before supper Mom?"

"Yes, just one slice."

His slippers were always in the spot where he left them, under the buffet table in the dining room. After putting them on, he washed his hands and face, ready for dinner: lamb stew with string beans and potatoes in a tomato sauce. A little bit of Italian bread- mm- a meal fit for a king!

He sat and had dinner with his family and discussed whether there would be school tomorrow if the snow persisted.

"I hope we have school tomorrow."

"Why is that, honey?"

"I have a big test in modern history, and I want to get it over with."

"Let's hope the snow stops for many reasons; not the least of which, my getting to work in the morning."

"I don't think there's going to be any school tomorrow, Dad."

"Maybe it will stop before midnight."

They had their dinner, talked about the snow and the problematic night it presented. He had his demitasse coffee and watched a special by Walter Cronkite on their 6 inch black and white TV.

When it was time for "I Love Lucy" George called, "Come on, "I Love Lucy's" on." They rushed into the living room and sat on the sofa next to him to watch the show. It was their favorite. They rolled with laughter. "That Lucy's so funny." Chuckled Virginia

She and their daughter went to bed around 10:00, George stayed to watch some more TV. After a while, he looked outside, and noticed the snow had stopped. He decided to go out and shovel before it froze. The night was crisp with a chill in the air. He put on his coat, boots, gloves, scarf and hat, opened the garage door, and began to shovel the driveway with only the light from the front of the house and the street lamp. He took stock of his life as he lifted each shovel of snow. He looked up at his house and thought 'This is mine. This is my home." His chest filled with pride. As he pushed the shovel into the next pile of snow he thought. 'How lucky I am to be here, shoveling the snow that

I never saw as a kid. My family is snug and warm in their beds in a home that I own. When he finished the driveway, he looked up at the sky saw the stars were bright like crystals, and he began to take deep breaths before starting on the sidewalk. The wind, at this moment, whipped the cold snow in to his face. Each scoop of snow became more difficult, and he began to labor with each push and pull.

Now with each scoop he thought again of his home, his children and his wife. How lucky he was. None of this could be if he hadn't come to this country and found his wife. The women are safe in their beds; no one will come and hurt them. 'I can stretch my legs to the end of my bed; no one will come and take my life from me or my family. If only my parents could see how far I've come.'

'I think I'd better stop. I'm really getting tired.' He felt as if he just couldn't do anymore. 'Ah, that's enough.' He was worn out. He looked up at the slow moving clouds, occasionally catching a glimpse of the moon. He could see the outline of the dark side and the other side was light. He thought, 'That's me. I came from the dark side of the moon and emerged through the light. Yes, that's me.'

He thumped the shovel into the ground to remove the excess snow and rested it up against the inside wall of the garage, closed the garage door and slowly walked up the three stairs and opened the door leading to the back hallway. He removed his boots and outer clothing, and decided to watch some TV before retiring.

He sat on the sofa to rest his body and to rest his eyes, letting the peace of the moment envelop him like a blanket. It was midnight and the station was signing off with the "Star Spangled Banner". He put his head back and tears came to his eyes when he heard the national anthem. He whispered, 'I love this country, I had a second chance because of you.' With those reflective thoughts and his heart overflowing with gratitude, his eyes remained closed for evermore.

"The Ending"

> *And did you get what you wanted from this life, even so?*
> *I did.*
> *And what did you want?*
> *To call myself beloved, to feel myself beloved, to feel myself beloved on the earth.*
>   *~Raymond Carver*

Chapter 24

Years after his death Virginia was in ill health, and she felt compelled to write a letter to her daughter explaining their early beginnings.

My Dearest Daughter Gloria,

I am writing this letter to you so you will understand our plight in our early years. I know when I was young I felt my mother and father's lives revolved around me and my siblings. I felt my parents only lived for me, and I never thought about their having a life when they were young. But they did have a life, and your dad and I also had a life.

Your father witnessed his parents' murder which affected his life forever. The way in which they died could never be erased from his mind. He lived in a refugee camp in Marseille for several years before coming to this country. My father died the day we arrived at Ellis Island which was traumatic. We struggled immeasurably without him. I stood up to my family to marry the man I loved, breaking all Greek tradition. But only in America could I have done this. If we lived in Greece, I would have married someone my family chose for me or never married at all. Your father accomplished so much in his short life. He learned tailoring at a young age. He opened his own successful business, and did it all on his own; never asking anything from anyone. But as he would say, "Only in America could I have what I have."

How he loved this country! For example, on Veteran's Day he closed the store and took us to watch the parade in Hartford. Do you remember that? He would carry you on his shoulders so you would have a better view. When the flag passed he put his hand over his heart. His heart filled with thankfulness, so proud of his country and grateful to those who served. Living here he knew anything and everything was possible. "Freedom, that's what America gave me, freedom." How many times he said that to me; how many times?

Do you remember when you were very young, every summer he closed the store for two weeks and rented a cottage at the beach? He wanted us to have everything he could afford.

I married your father over the objections of my family. Not only was he not from our part of Greece, but he wasn't even Greek. It was a bittersweet existence at the beginning, but as my family got to know him, they loved him. There wasn't anything your dad wouldn't do for anyone in my family. I want you to know that.

I think my undying love for him and the joy you and your brother brought him, gave him sustenance and stability. That he died so young was tragic. But I know he felt a sense of pride and success.

I hope this letter explains a little about us and our beginnings. Every parent wants their children to have a better life than they; and that's what I wish for you. Be proud of who you are and from where your family came. You are Greek and Armenian. We're fortunate to be Americans, but also proud of our rich heritage.

All my love,

Mom

"Life is for the living, so live it and love living it."
~Virginia Mollis Avak

A NOTE FROM THE AUTHOR

It wasn't until I started writing the book that I fully understood my father's plight. The sadness, the tears, the unhappiness he displayed throughout his life now made sense to me, as I wrote. Only my mother, with her humor and positive attitude could coax him back to the present.

He died when I was fifteen. Until then I thought of only myself and believed my parents lived just for my brother and me. As the years went on, I became more intrigued about their young lives. Then I knew I had to write the book.

From my parent's union, their two children married, gave them five grandchildren and twelve great grandchildren.

ACKNOWLEDGMENTS

My husband Jim Pitchell for his love, encouragement and always being there for me.

My Editor and Beta Reader, Janet Grevstad, who is always willing to share her knowledge with me.

My Second Beta Reader, Dorothy Graham, who's kind words will always be with me.

My Writers' Circle friends: Bobbie Coughlin, Sandra Diamond, Liz Kirkpatrick, Martha Mayer, Trevann Rogers, Diane Shovak and Sara Strecker, who shared my journey and gave me the impetus to finish the book.

A Special Thank you to Elizabeth Garner who taught me to abandon my fear and make my writing the best it can be.

To Sara Strecker, for her assistance in helping me publish my book, and using her creativity and expertise in many different areas, including helping me create the cover.

To my cousins: George Andrews, Joan Clarke and Jean Spargo for their recollections and constant interest in the development of the book.

To my brother, George Avak, who shares in our parent's legacy.

213

To my granddaughter, Taylor Pitchell, who, one night, looked up at the sky and said, "Yiayia, I can see the dark and the light side of the moon." Then, I immediately realized that that was going to be the title of my book, as it captured the essence of my story.

About the Author

Gloria Avak Pitchell is a professional artist, vocalist, dancer, and pianist. She has written short stories and poems and this is her first novel. She studied Radiology at Saint Francis Hospital School of Radiology and studied music at Julius Hartt School of Music and painting (oil and acrylic) with Ms. Theresa Cosma and dancing with Ms. Frances Deeley. She has worked as a professional placement consultant and lives in Wethersfield, Connecticut with her husband and has two married sons and six grandchildren.

BIBLIOGRAPHY

A Guide to Greek Traditions and Customs in America by Marilyn Rouvelas

Armenian Genocide Resource Center

National Park Service – U.S. Department of the Interior

My Reading Life by Pat Conroy

Not Even My Name by Thea Halo

The Black Dog of Fate by Peter Balakian

The Forty Days of Musa Dagh from Wikipedia

The Man I Love by George and Ira Gershwin

The Sand Castle Girls by Chris Buhjalian

Made in the USA
Middletown, DE
31 May 2015